FALLING

~A FARAWAY HIGH FAIRYTALE~

SCARLETT KOL

The characters in this book are fictitious. Any similarity to real persons, living or dead, places, or events is coincidental and not intended by author.

FALLING
Copyright © 2019 by Scarlett Kol

ISBN: (ebook) 978-1-7752260-1-7
Print: 978-1-7752260-0-0
First Edition: 2019

Edited by Laura Parnum
www.LauraParnumBooks.com

Author Photo by Regina Wamba

Published by Vicious Pixie Press

To those who believe in fairytales and following their hearts.

To Constance,
Believe in magic!
Scarlett
Kol

"Yes, you are dearest of all to me," said the Prince, "for you have the best heart of them all."

- Hans Christian Anderson,
The Little Mermaid

Translated: M. R. James (1862-1936)

1

*O*nce upon a time, someone said "Heaven knows no pain, because it knows no sin." This person lied. Or maybe they'd just been misquoted and in need of a better publicist, because I'd definitely sinned up here, and as I waited outside the Court of Heaven for my name to be called, my knotted stomach hurt more than an eternity of torture in Hell.

It's not like I'd committed a big sin. I didn't murder anyone or steal anything, but if any transgression against divine law counted as sin, then yep, I was guilty. Guilty. Guilty. Guilty.

I tapped my foot nervously on the marble tile. The steady sound of it echoed throughout the great hall, bouncing off the intricately frescoed ceilings and rattling the gilded candelabras. Beside the grand doorway to the inner court, the two guards eyed my drumming foot, then looked at each other with matching annoyed sneers, but I really didn't care. Angels of my class weren't often called before the court, so they needed to get over my anxiety. If only I could too.

The bolt on the door banged as it unlocked, and the guards turned at attention, ready for whatever might come storming through. Instead, the door slowly creaked open, just enough for the court recorder, Malachi, to slip out.

"Arianna," he said. "Raguel would like to see you now." His expression revealed nothing, his disciplined gaze flat and unreadable. Years of working as an officer had dulled his ability to emote and provide any glimpse of what lay before me beyond the doors.

I gulped and stood up from the tiny marble bench. My legs shook, threatening to give out and leave me flailing on the cold stone floor. I closed my eyes and tried to slow my breathing, counting backward from ten as I straightened my gown and fluffed up my wings. If I had to go on trial, I should at least look my best. I doubted it would help, but I had few options left.

The guards grabbed the iron door handles and pushed them inward to let me pass. I studied the intricate carvings in the wood panels, trying to avoid looking forward. Each tableau depicted justice being carried out, swift and heartless as was its way. Slaughtered felons and severed heads littered the artwork and I took a deep breath, hoping I wouldn't one day join them. Especially not today.

I'd barely taken a few steps into the court when the guards slammed the door shut with a thunderous boom, nearly nipping my heels. A few pure white feathers fell from my wings in the abrupt draft and drifted softly to the ground.

"Arianna, please step forward."

Raguel stood at the end of the aisle, before the benches of the court, his arms stretched out toward me. Radiant light beamed off his azure robes, almost inviting, almost safe, unless you knew what you were walking into. Raguel, the high angel of justice. A gentle soul, but with the ability to bring the strongest men and divine to their knees. The angel who'd struck down armies in their boots. Without hesitation. Without remorse.

Rows of angels sat along the edges of the aisle, sad eyes and shaking heads, here to see my fate. I avoided their heavy stares as I trudged farther into the court. Their condemnation weighed down upon my shoulders as I walked.

"You are accused of breaking the cardinal rule of your kind. What say you?"

I swallowed, carefully reviewing my words again in my head. I'd practiced them a thousand times, but now, standing in this place, they didn't seem appropriate. Didn't seem enough. I laced my hands behind my back and ran my fingertips along the downy softness of my feathers, hoping the familiar would bring me strength.

"I think this has all been a big misunderstanding."

Raguel shook his head. His long platinum strands rippled in waves that flowed gently over his shoulders like a waterfall. Everything about him, from the top of his stunning head to the bottoms of his strong and sturdy feet, radiated with an unnatural beauty. A beauty that could swiftly turn lethal if crossed unprepared.

"Did you not change the course of fate for one—" he

turned toward the angels on the court and after hushed whispers turned back, "—Henry Tatum?"

The moment spun in a loop in my brain. The carousel of misdeeds that a certain Henry Tatum had committed. Over and over he'd made the same bad decisions, affecting all those around him. For once, he needed to break the cycle of those bad decisions and pay penance for his ill-lived life. I could no longer let him destroy his family and those who loved him, unaware or unwilling to believe what he was capable of. In that moment, the one in which I intervened and punished Henry, my heart did not feel shame. It did not feel guilt. It seemed the exact right decision.

"Yes and no."

Raguel smirked and crossed his arms over his chest. His gold-tipped wings shone in the light, making him appear even more holy, even more terrifying. "Explain."

"I'd been watching Mr. Tatum, and it was merely a matter of time before he received comeuppance for his misdeeds. I simply speeded up the process to avoid any further harm to anyone else."

"Did you, now? Or did you make things worse?"

I scanned the faces on the court, each one hanging off his words, waiting for mine. Except I had none of my own to respond.

"What if you hadn't inserted yourself into Mr. Tatum's life, and he moved on to make better decisions? His wife was pregnant. Did you know that? What if after the birth of the child he became a changed man?"

"And what if he didn't?" I blurted, immediately covering my mouth with my hand for talking out of line.

These were the things that constantly kept me in trouble. Never knowing when enough was enough.

He nodded for me to continue.

I swallowed hard. "What if, instead, he continued down the same path and made the same awful decisions? Or worse—endangered his wife and his child?"

"Do you not believe in the power of love as redemption?"

I stopped and thought over my words. I couldn't lie. Not before the court.

"In this case, I don't. I don't believe that love could be strong enough to fix him. To change his path."

The collective gasped, and I clenched my eyes shut, knowing my mouth had run away with me again. "I think he would have destroyed everyone around him."

"But that would have been his choice. Humans were gifted free will—the ability to make their own decisions regardless of outcome. We are not meant to override those decisions or circumstances."

Raguel hung his head and began to pace in front of the court. My knees quivered beneath my gown, fighting the urge to run out of the room and never return. Maybe I could hide amongst the stars and disappear, or fly off to a distant planet where no one would ever find me. Except, they would. Heaven's reach surpassed all limits of my potential fugitive imagination.

"So, you stand here, doubting the gifts bestowed on humankind by our Lord—love and free will."

"I don't—"

"Silence," Raguel shouted, raising his hand in the air. The entire room fell deathly quiet. "I no longer wish to hear argument. Even ignoring these facts, what is the single most important rule among the angels?"

I stared down at the floor, my chin nearly hitting my chest. "Do not interfere with humankind."

"I didn't hear you."

"Do not interfere with the humans," I said louder, my hands clenched into fists at my side.

"And did you interfere with humans?"

"Yes."

"And is this the first time you've been warned about interfering?"

I hung my head again as my shoulders rose. "No."

The room erupted in a flurry of accusations and chaos, but I kept my eyes locked on the veins of gray in the shiny marble floor. I tried to block out the voices, but each one wound my muscles tighter, bit by bit like harp strings being tuned, as my body begged to collapse in on itself. To implode. To vanish.

"Enough," Raguel yelled, and calm resumed.

He walked toward me and placed his hands upon my cheeks, holding both my face and my stare. "I do not believe you intended harm, but divine law has been broken and you must receive punishment. If you doubt the gifts bestowed on humans, then maybe the best lesson would be to walk among them."

I squirmed in his grip, but he held firm. "You want me to go to Earth?"

"Yes, but not as an angel. As a human. If you do not understand humanity, then it's best you learn. Seven days. I give you seven days to discover the truth of humanity, or you shall not return to Heaven."

"Understand humanity? What does that mean?"

"That is for you to find out. It is not enough just to walk among them. You need to actually experience—be human. Feel as they feel, live as they live, learn as you need to."

"But what if I fail?"

Raguel removed his hands and walked back to the front of the court. "I suggest you don't. But if you do not succeed, you are no longer welcome here. So I have said, so shall it be done."

He clapped his hands twice and the room began to spin. I reached out, grasping for anything that would keep me still, but my fingers simply slipped through the empty air. A sharp searing pain scalded the top of my shoulder blades and tore across my back as the weight of my wings disappeared. The rest of my skin ignited, set afire with agony, raw and deep. I reached behind me. A sticky wetness coated my fingers and I pulled my hand forward again, dripping splotches of dark red blood. I screamed. Pain pulsed through my body, ripping every part of me and forcing it back together again. The light mixed with the dark, mixed with the nothing, and I lost my grip on the floor. My stomach rose into my throat as gravity took hold.

And then, I fell.

2

*A*ll Raguel had left me was pain. Pain and darkness.

My head ached. At the back of my skull and in the space just behind my eyes, pressure built like my brain might explode. Fortunately, I'd stayed still long enough for the fiery sting across my shoulder blades to finally be extinguished, but it had now been replaced by an irritating itch, deep within my flesh and impossible to scratch. I stretched out my limbs, fighting against the burning and throbbing in my joints that made every movement more awful than the last. If this was humanity, it sucked.

I eased my eyes open. The world lay still, bathed in dark with only the speckles of stars in the sky. Except these weren't the majestic inspiring beacons that stars should be. Just unrecognizable blobs breaking up the infinite night. How sad. I sat up, the motion ripping through my human veins, unnatural and unyielding. I reached my hand behind my back and concentrated, waiting for my silken feathers to brush against my fingers, but they didn't. My stomach hollowed. *This is real now.*

I struggled to my feet, my knees quaking, threatening to toss me back down to the dirty ground. Death surrounded me. Scorch marks stretched across the ground from where I stood, exploded out like a firework. All life—every blade of grass—crunched beneath my feet, charred to a dark crisp. Just beyond the touchdown point, the world continued again. Fields, maybe a meadow with green grass and purple asters, drooped in the night, waiting for the radiant sun to wake them again.

"Must've been some trip."

I spun around to follow the voice, a deep cadence with an edge of a chuckle. *I'll teach them to laugh at my predicament.* But my head kept spinning after my feet stopped and I buckled over, grabbing my knees, hoping for the world to stay still. The voice—a man—rushed over and tossed a thin blanket across my back as he threw my arm over his shoulder, taking my full weight.

"Easy now. It's going to take a little while to get adjusted. Humans are complicated, but I'm sure you'll figure that out."

We walked over the singed earth. The fire that happened here seared through the bottoms of my feet, sparking every nerve up through the back of my spine. I leaned into the man. The evening breeze rustled through his grayed hair. Whispers of peppermint and orange rolled off his skin and helped calm the thoughts flooding through my brain, all of them moving too fast to focus on any in particular.

Soon the fresh life of the meadow bent under my footsteps. The cool dew eased the pain, although every step still seemed detached from my body. Foreign. Unfamiliar. Human.

Ahead, a dirt road rose out of the field. A green car with its lights shining off into the distance sat with the doors open, waiting. I charged toward the car, the lights propelling me forward, teasing out my last bit of strength. The man by my side struggled to keep up but held firm to my shoulder, not letting my will overpower my ability. As we approached, an older woman stepped out of the passenger seat with her arms full of clothes and a broad smile across her face.

"In you go."

I settled into the back seat as the man wrenched his shoulder back in a circle, stretching out the strain. The burden of holding me up. The woman patted him on the cheek and he kissed her forehead. A gentle glow surrounded the two of them for a moment before it disappeared into the dark.

"Here you are, love. I hope they fit. Been a while since I've had to shop for an angel on such short notice." She leaned into the open car door and rested the pile of clothes on my lap. Her smile stretched wider, revealing cracks of concern around the edges that echoed in her eyes. "And there's some food in the basket on the seat. Make sure to drink the water. Even the strongest get dehydrated after a fall like that."

"Who . . . who are you?" The words tripped up my throat and rolled out, unrefined and blunt.

"Margaret and James Danley. Pleased to meet you." She stuck her hand in front of me, and I took it. A

warm tingle flowed from her soft skin, easing my
defenses.

"And—"

"Earth, dear. Just outside Faraway. Iowa. The
Hawkeye State."

Iowa? Where in the world was Iowa?

Margaret retrieved her hand and closed the door
with a thunk, then took a seat in the front of the car.
James settled behind the steering wheel and turned on
the engine. A lilting melody and a powerful female voice
exploded from the radio as the car moved down the
road. I slid into the borrowed baggy pants and hooded
sweatshirt, the rough cotton itchy against my raw skin.

As the car bumped along the highway, I dug into the
basket on the seat beside me. The delicious smells of
food blasted at my face as I opened the lid. My stomach
curled and twisted, my body finally relaxing enough to
let the hunger take hold. I opened the bottle of water
and downed the contents in three insatiable gulps,
numbing the ash-covered desert that burned the inside
of my throat. I filled my mouth with meat and cheese
and fruit, every morsel seeming better and more deca-
dent than the one before. James peeked back at me in
the rearview mirror and chuckled to himself, likely
never having seen a divine acting this savage before. But
I didn't care. Easing my aching hunger outweighed the
negative opinion of a random stranger.

"How did you know where to find me?" I settled
back in my seat, the gluttonous feast landing in the
bottom of my stomach, heavy but still satisfying.

"Oh, it wasn't that hard, you know, with the blazing
blue streak plummeting out of the sky and all." James

gave a hearty laugh and Margaret placed a hand on his shoulder, shaking her head. "Plus, Margaret could see you."

"See me?" I gripped the edge of the seat as my fingernails dug into the cracked leather seat, unsure who or what I'd simply let take me away.

"Yes, dear. My eyesight hasn't been fantastic for a long while, but the visions are still clear as a bell." Margaret turned back to face me, the small white spots on her left eye now visible under the interior lights. "We are messengers. We see things regular mortals can't, and then we help where we can. And before you ask, no, you aren't our first angel."

I wiped my hand over my forehead. Margaret's ability to predict my thoughts left me feeling exposed. Could she read my mind, or had she done this enough times to just know?

"How old—I mean . . . how long have you been doing this?"

James chuckled again. "I don't know. What's it been, Maggie? Six or seven hundred years?"

She gave James a sweet smile, memories broadcasting across her face. "It's been a while, let's just put it that way. But enough about us, what brings you here?"

I closed my eyes, pieces flooding back into my brain. The marble flooring. The judgments. The weightlessness as the ground beneath my feet shifted and the world I knew fell away. "I'm here to learn about humanity. If I don't, I'll lose my wings forever."

James emitted a high-pitched whistle through his teeth. "Well that's quite the dilemma you have there. Must've been some crime for that type of punishment."

"Or maybe they were just being too harsh?"

"Or maybe you have a lot to learn, young lady?"

I shuddered and looked out the window. *Young lady?* I'd been around longer than his human brain could even imagine. I propped my elbow on the door and rested my cheek on my fist. The highway changed from open fields to small houses flying past, dotted in perfect little lines. Soon the car slowed and pulled into the crooked drive of a narrow bungalow-style house, its sky-blue paint peeling and weathered around the windows and doors.

"Where are we?"

James adjusted the rearview mirror, his green eyes catching my face in the reflection.

"Your new home."

3

The car halted and James jumped out of the front seat, then scurried around the car to open my door. The residual hunger pangs in the bottom of my stomach twisted into something darker, more on edge. I stepped out, the gravel crunching beneath the ratty sandals Margaret had graciously provided. I looked at James and then the house and back again.

"How long have you lived here?"

"Oh, no. We don't live here. Our job is just to help you on your way. The rest is up to you." James opened the trunk of the car and struggled to retrieve a large burgundy suitcase. I rushed over to help, but he waved me off, his face glowing crimson in the dark as he lowered it to the ground.

I glanced at the house again and a flash of black brushed past my face. I jumped back, banging my shoulder into the side of the car. *Ow!* I rubbed the sore spot and watched the black crow perch on the small garden fence that edged the driveway. It flapped its slick, pitch-dark feathers then cocked its little head to the side and stared at me with beady red eyes. I looked away, bunching the cuffs of the borrowed sweater into my hands. The crow made a shrill cawing sound. I straightened my stance and exhaled. How would I ever figure out humans if I could be this rattled by a common bird?

James closed the trunk lid and rushed at the crow, flapping his arms in the air. "You get out of here, now," he shouted, until the crow flew off, squawking at James as it ascended and disappeared into the dark night. He clearly wasn't a big fan of birds either.

The screen door of the house slammed in its casing, and two shadows appeared on the porch.

"Come on, now." James shuffled behind me with the suitcase. His gentle fingertips in the center of my back prodded me forward and provided the courage I desperately lacked in that moment.

At the front door stood a man, younger than James—but I guess most mortal men would be—and a girl, even younger, with similar close-set eyes and narrow nose as the man's. Perhaps a daughter or niece.

"Good evening, Stephen." James rushed around me and marched up the front steps, his arm extended.

Stephen took his hand as a weary smile broke across his lips. "Nice to see you again."

"This here is . . ." he held out his arm to me, but a puzzled look quickly settled across his face. "Forgive an old man, I don't quite remember your name."

I crossed my arms against my chest. "Arianna. My name is Arianna."

James snapped his fingers and his head jerked forward. "That's right. Arianna Fell."

I snickered. *Very clever, James.*

"Well, it's a pleasure to meet you," Stephen said, putting his hands on his hips as the girl stepped around the adults. "And this here is my daughter, Chloe."

She rushed down the stairs, her wavy hair bouncing over her shoulders.

"Nice to meet you." She stuck out her hand for me to shake as her friendly gaze scanned me over, scrutinizing, or maybe simply assessing this new being in her space.

I took her hand and shook. The men looked on with pride as though they'd been responsible for this pleasant encounter.

"James says you're a senior, just like me. I'll be able to show you everything there is to know about Faraway High."

"High school?" I croaked the words as they stuck in my throat, all sharp and prickly. I knew Raguel had planned to punish me, but high school? He might as well have sent me straight to the pits of Hell.

I STOOD ALONE on the front steps as James and Margaret pulled out of the driveway and their red taillights disappeared around the corner. Gulping a deep breath of night air, I paused, letting the oxygen circulate through my bloodstream, mentally preparing myself to go into the house and meet another set of new people that I didn't understand. Were these all tasks Raguel had planned, or were they just a series of events to put a roof over my head and keep me from starving? At least he'd shown me some mercy. He could've dropped me broken, naked, and starving on a street corner. I should've been gracious for those small miracles, but I couldn't help the anger still boiling up inside.

I entered the quaint kitchen and clicked the screen door shut behind me. Stephen stood in the center of the room, squared stance as if waiting for me to come in, while Chloe sat on the countertop, her legs swinging just above the floor.

"Please have a seat." Stephen gestured at the rustically carved wooden chair in front of me and sat down in the one across the table from it.

"No thanks. I'd rather stand." I crossed my arms. There wasn't any reason not to follow directions, but falling from the sky and crash landing in a field had suddenly evoked the need to be insubordinate. Besides, who knew what I was in for.

Stephen ran his hands through his salt-and-pepper hair then placed them folded on the table, fidgeting with a tarnished silver ring on his left hand.

"Have it your way. I know it's late, and I know you've probably had a very long day, so I will ignore the attitude for now. However, if you expect to live in this house—no matter how short the time frame—you are expected to behave accordingly. I don't ask for much, simply helping around the house, watching your language, and showing some respect. Do you think you can handle that?"

I opened my mouth to argue, the words ripe on the tip of my tongue, but nothing came out. From another man with another temperament, that speech would've sent me marching right out the door, but Stephen didn't appear to be that guy. The lines etched across his forehead and around his eyes crinkled with a warm kindness. He wasn't my enemy. He'd been generous enough to take in a wayward angel and simply wanted no trouble. Not an unreasonable request.

I nodded, still refusing to sit but allowing my arms to fall to my side.

"So, we're in agreement then. It's great to meet you, Arianna. Please make yourself at home."

"Thank you." As I opened my mouth, the words came out muffled, mixed with a yawn that stretched my mouth to what felt like the size of my entire head.

"Looks like you can use some sleep. We can discuss more in the morning." He stood and tapped his knuckles twice on the table top then turned to his daughter. "Chloe? Please show our guest to the spare room."

Chloe launched off the countertop and scampered across the kitchen, down a narrow hallway. "Come on."

I looked Stephen over one last time, still unsure about what exactly had transpired tonight, but at least the uncomfortable pain of alarm had let go of my chest.

"One more thing," he said. "I expect you to stay on top of your studies. There is no cutting classes in this house."

Class? I doubted the answers to discovering the truth of humanity would be conveniently stated in any textbook, but that was a problem I needed to solve tomorrow. My head had started to swim, and exhaustion coursed through my limbs.

I made my way down the hallway to where Chloe stood beside an open door. She stepped aside to let me pass into a tiny bedroom, then followed behind with the battered suitcase James had left.

"So where are you from?"

"Excuse me?" I shook my head, distracted by the floral bedspread, the tiny flowers drifting in circles as I struggled to keep standing on my tired feet.

"I said, where are you from?"

James hadn't given me a backstory. I probably should have spent more time considering that on the drive here. But no one had left me a manual on what I needed to do.

"Um . . . city . . . angel . . . Angel city." *Well, that was awful.*

"So, like, Los Angeles?"

I narrowed my stare, trying to understand the words coming out of her bow-shaped mouth.

"You know, the City of Angels. Los Angeles."

"Yeah, right. Definitely, that's where I'm from. Los Angeles." I put my hand on my forehead and rubbed it over my face. "Sorry, just a little out of it right now."

"That's so cool. I've never been to a big city like that before."

"Well, maybe . . ." another yawn breached past my lips ". . . one day."

Chloe giggled, nice and light, and even though I didn't understand why, I laughed with her.

"I better let you get some sleep. We can talk more tomorrow." She grinned and nodded, as if her mind were already devising a plan for me. "Good night, Arianna."

"Good night."

I waved as she bounced out of the room and back up the hall. She seemed sweet, but I'd yet to determine if she could be trusted. I sat down on the bed and looked around the room. Nothing more than a bed and dresser with my lumpy luggage in the middle of the floor. I glanced in the mirror above the dresser. I looked dreadful. The glow around me had faded, and dark purple circles had formed under my eyes. Would I ever be myself again?

In front of the mirror sat a tiny silver frame. I picked it up and ran my fingertips over the three people in the photo, tracing the outlines of their heads. Stephen stood on the left of the frame and Chloe in the middle—but not as themselves now—as they were three or four years ago. Chloe's wide smile and the two thick braids hanging down the side of her head made her look even younger, but her face seemed closer to today's Chloe than that of a child. The third person stood on the right. A woman. The same sunny blond hair as Chloe's, but with softer features. Maybe this was her mother, or possibly another relative of some sort, otherwise it would be impossible for two people to have such a similar smile.

I put down the photo and lay down on the bed. Tomorrow would be a new day and a new start, but I still didn't know what I was looking for. Maybe once the clouds moved out of my sleepy brain, I would find the sun.

4

---

*T*he traitorous sun prickled against my skin, threatening to strike me blind the moment I dared to open my eyes. I defied its wrath and kept them shut, stretching my arms above my head and extending my legs until sharp tingles crept up my thighs. Good pain. The ache of falling still screamed in my joints, but if I ever planned on getting home again, I'd have to get over it. I wrapped my arms around the pillow beneath my head and rolled onto my side where the rays of sunshine couldn't catch me.

Blood pumped strong in my veins again, the thumping of my own human heart almost lulling me back to slumber. Rest made sense to me. All bodies needed time to recuperate once in a while. But sleep— sleep seemed frivolous. Although clearly a necessary part of functioning, the thought that mortals spent half their lives not living them seemed wasteful. No wonder they made such bad decisions. They missed so many hours of experience.

"Shoot."

I whipped open my eyes and screamed at a face mere inches from mine. The face screamed back and fell into a pile on the floor. I scrambled to a sitting position and crawled backward until my elbow smashed into the wall. *Ouch!* I rubbed my elbow and peeked over the edge of the bed to see Chloe steadying herself on crouched legs and grabbing sheets of fluffy gray fabric from the floor. She stood up and folded the fabric into neat rectangles and placed them on the dresser.

"I'm sorry." She rubbed her hand over her face, the fresh crimson color draining from her cheeks. "I didn't mean to scare you. I just came to bring you some clean towels, but I tripped and dropped them."

I exhaled, letting the pent-up sensation flow out of my chest through my mouth. I slid back toward the other side of the bed and let my feet hang over the side, my toes brushing the cold floor.

"It's all right. I guess I'm just still a little jumpy. New home and all."

"Yeah, I'm sure I'd never know what to do if I had to start over with a new family." Chloe brushed her bangs away from her face. The morning light picked up hints of gold in each strand of her hair and created an ethereal glow around her. Almost like the divine ones back home. Almost, but not quite.

"Your dad seems nice, but what about the rest of your family? Do you have brothers and sisters?"

She shook her head.

"What about your mom? Will I meet her today?"

Chloe's face paled and she turned away. She ran her fingertips over the fussy carpentry work on the edges of the dresser, her nails scratching at the fake gold trim. "No, it's just us. Dad and me."

"I'm sorry." My rib cage gripped tightly around my lungs and my breath caught in my throat, creating a deep burn in my chest. I nodded toward the photo to her left. The happy trio. "I just thought . . ."

"It's okay. We get along fine." Her body quaked, then a forced smile broke across her face. "Besides, my life is super boring. I want to hear more about you."

Me? "Uh . . . what did James and Margaret tell you?"

"Not much. Just that they knew someone in need and asked if we were willing to help."

"Just like that? You must trust them. How well do you know them, really? I mean, do you know *all* about them?"

Chloe's stare narrowed and she wrinkled her nose, either taking in my words or analyzing them. She clearly didn't know the whole truth, and I'd opened up a hidden door. Either that or this high school girl could lie better than a demon.

"Seems like I'm a lot to take on with only limited information."

"They've been good to us. They've belonged to our church as long as I can remember, and any time we've ever needed anything, they've gone out of their way to help. It was a simple favor for all the good things they've done."

"Your church? Wait, it's Sunday morning. You're not skipping just to keep an eye on me, are you?"

She laughed. "No. Dad's there now, but I haven't gone since . . ." The lightness drained from her expression. "For a few years." Then she grinned slyly.

"Besides, you don't seem as bad as you make yourself out to be."

"Thanks a lot." I grabbed the pillow and chucked it across the room, barely missing Chloe's shoulder. She pivoted and avoided the attack, her voice tinkling like bells as she giggled at my pathetic throw.

"Seriously though, what did you do to end up here? Steal things? Drugs? You don't look like a drug addict to me, but I don't know that many either. Or at least I don't think I do. Did you hurt someone?" She took a slight step back—so slow and careful as if to ensure I didn't notice—and her eyes darted toward the open door.

I stood up. Chloe's hands wrapped into fists, her muscles clenching as she shifted her weight to her toes.

"No, I didn't hurt anyone. I just . . . I helped someone I shouldn't have. I thought I'd done the right thing, but my family disagreed with me." The disappointment on Raguel's face seared across my brain, and I cringed. "So, they kicked me out."

Chloe studied my face, running her eyes over every feature as if trying to find a crack in my story. Then her lips turned up on the right in a sympathetic smile. "Sounds like a bit of an overreaction to me."

"I know, right? They're just really strict and don't take well to broken rules."

"Well, until they come to their senses, you are welcome to stay with us. We have rules too, but it sounds like it'll be a lot easier than where you've come from."

"Thank you, Chloe. You're a really kind soul."

Her cheeks flushed. "I try, but I wouldn't go around talking like that. People will think you're weird. I mean

—I don't—I just want you to have a good experience here." She gazed down at the floor, fighting the smile attempting to burst across her lips, then peeked up at me through her long lashes. "Besides, I've kind of always wanted a sister, even if it's just for a little while."

"I'd be honored. But I don't think I'll be here that long."

She shrugged. "I'll take what I can get."

"Now, where do you find the humans on a Sunday in Iowa?"

"What?" Chloe's face twisted in confusion.

Humans. Right. Shouldn't really refer to them like that.

"I mean, where the people are. Where do people like to go? I'd like to get acquainted with this town as quickly as possible."

"The farmer's market, I guess. Most people go to the big ones in the city on Saturdays, but our local one is Sunday afternoons."

"Perfect. Then let's go." I nodded and headed toward the door, the adrenaline from getting started on my quest prickling underneath my skin.

"Um . . ."

I spun around, but Chloe hadn't followed.

"What?" I looked down, taking in the printed flannel flamingos splattered across the pajamas I'd found in the burgundy suitcase last night. "Oh, right. I should probably get changed."

"Yeah, and you might want to shower. You still have some dirt . . ." She brushed her hand along her cheek and her neck.

I mimicked her gesture, the grit of dried mud rough

under my fingertips. "Of course. I should probably take care of that."

Chloe grabbed one of the folded towels from the dresser and held it out for me. "If you ever feel like telling me how that happened, I'm sure I'd love to hear it."

5

*T*he cool fall breeze swirled the gold and cinnamon leaves across the gravel lot leading into the market field. I pulled my sweater sleeves down and bunched them in my palms as the tiny hairs on my neck prickled straight up. Although the fabric itched a little against my skin, Margaret had done a great job picking out the wardrobe she'd left for me in the suitcase. Most items were plain, but they blended in well with the other girls in town. I didn't need to call any extra attention to myself. What would these people do if they knew an angel walked among them? But without my wings, was I even an angel anymore?

"Welcome to the Faraway Farmer's Market. Is it everything you hoped it would be?" Chloe spread her arm in front of her and led me into the throng of people buzzing between the rows of tiny tents and market stalls.

She linked her arm in mine and jerked her head toward the vendors. "C'mon."

We maneuvered through the crowd, expertly avoiding the stray arms and elbows of the other patrons and the lineups that extended deep into the distance. We passed apples, corn, and other odd-shaped fruits and vegetables I'd never seen before piled high in crates. Soaps, honeys, and sweet treats packaged with homemade flair lined tables serviced by smiley-faced women hoping to sell just one more lemon loaf. The rich scent of popcorn and caramel squeezed through the cracks between the bodies, as if beckoning us onward like sirens of scent instead of song.

On the far side of the field the crowd thinned, and young people milled about, trying desperately not to be involved with the chaos.

"Chloe." A tall girl ran up to us and pulled Chloe into a hug. "I didn't think you were coming because of your new guest."

At the words "new guest," the girl had made matching peace sign gestures with her hands then bent them at the knuckles as a sly smirk whispered across her lips. Clearly, this girl had mocked me, but I didn't understand the punchline.

"Actually, she wanted to come." Chloe pulled me forward to stand in front of the mystery girl. "Stace, meet Arianna."

"Hi," the girl said, as a pink blush blossomed along her cheekbones. "You aren't at all what I expected."

"Nice, Stacey." Chloe elbowed her in the arm, and Stacey frowned. "What she means is that we figured you'd be a lot . . . rougher, I guess. The way James mentioned you, it seemed like you'd practically done hard time or something."

"Oh. So, everyone thinks I'm some sort of criminal?"

"No." Chloe took my hands and maneuvered herself in front of me so I couldn't avoid her emerald gaze. "I only told Stacey about you. Everything happened so fast, and I had no idea what to expect, so I hadn't really thought it through. I'm sorry." She bit on her bottom lip and her eyes widened, open and innocent. She meant it.

"It's fine, but maybe you can stick with a cousin or an exchange student or something?"

She nodded and then wrapped her arm around my shoulders. "Deal. Now you've already met Stacey, but over there," she pointed toward a group standing near the popcorn truck, "is Summer, Ashley, Conner, Nikki, Sasha, and Brad."

"I'm not going to remember all that."

"No worries. It's your first day. We don't have a test until mid-semester." She laughed and tugged me off toward the group.

"Everyone, this is . . . my cousin, Arianna."

I raised my hand and waved politely as they provided their welcomes and condolences for being trapped in small-town Iowa.

The novelty of my existence wore off quickly, and the conversation turned back to other things. Inside jokes and stories about people I'd never met. But being an outsider was exactly what I needed. To be able to sit back, observe, absorb. Besides, if all worked out, I'd be gone before anyone had the chance to know me anyway.

I listened to their conversations for a while, but the words droned on and swirled into each other. I wouldn't be able to figure out humanity through an endless loop of gossip. I tugged Chloe's arm and she turned to me with a wide smile.

"Having fun?"

"Of course," I lied, "but I've never been to a farmer's market before, so I'm going to go take a look around."

"For sure. Hey guys, I'm gonna jet."

"No," I shouted, then corrected my tone. "You don't need to come, I'll just look around and then I'll be right back. Don't let me take you away from your friends."

"Are you sure?" Her eyes questioned, almost as if they could see right through my lie.

I nodded, not risking any more words in the atmosphere. "I'll only be a few minutes. And besides," I pointed over at the fence that ran around the market grounds, "those crows are creeping me out. I feel like they're staring at me."

"Ha. You're not that special. They annoy everyone. But don't get too far. Wouldn't want you to wander off and die of boredom. There would be no one to save you."

"Right."

I faced back toward the crowd. Now or never. I needed to figure out what made these people who they were and learn whatever lesson Raguel needed to teach me or I'd never make my way back to Heaven. But what could these small-town mortals teach me that I couldn't learn when I had the ability of seeing all things?

Quickening my pace, I passed the crow-lined fence, the line of red eyes watching my every step. No wonder they called crows a "murder." The large one on the left looked like it wanted to rip my limbs from my body and use them to build its nest.

I moved along the tents, scanning the faces and trying to make sense of my task, but nothing stuck out. People bartered their goods and talked to their neighbors, while children played in corners with toys or lost themselves in the screens of tablets and cell phones where they wouldn't be a nuisance. Understand humanity? Humanity seemed like a big jumbled mess.

I stared up at the bright sky and let the warm sun heat my skin as I closed my eyes. *What did you want from me, Raguel? What is the lesson I'm supposed to learn? Can't you give me any sort of sign?*

Someone jostled me as they passed and I opened my eyes, grabbing the edge of the nearest table to avoid falling over. So much for signs.

Just ahead a young man—maybe nineteen or twenty—with patches of dark stubble across his jaw, moved through the crowd with odd jerky movements. He took quick, short steps, knocking into other patrons and then racing away. His head swiveled from side to side in frantic twitches. I followed close behind as he nearly upended a mother and her stroller, unsure why his erratic behavior intrigued me but intent on finding out.

About halfway through the rows of tents, he slipped between the tables and around to the back of one of the stalls. He stopped and crossed his left leg over the other, leaning against a table, casual and suddenly relaxed. I inched closer, picking up a stack of knitted dish cloths at the stall closest to him. I turned them over in my hands, trying not to look suspicious.

He slid down the edge of the table, farther away from the main flow of traffic, then looked back and forth. I glanced down as he scanned my direction, then watched as he crept into the stall and shoved handfuls of green bills in his open denim jacket.

"Hey, what are you doing?" I dropped the dish cloths and raced toward him.

He glanced up, his eyes wide and jaw open as he saw me coming for him. He jumped out of the stall, panic blanching his face, confirming that it wasn't his money to take.

I whipped around the corner as he raced down the back side of the tents where the crowd thinned. Every step of his long legs was two times the length of mine. If only I had my wings. I split my focus—half my energy in my feet to keep running and half between my shoulders on the rare chance my wings would materialize when I needed them. I pushed my body harder, trying to make my legs move faster as the thief stumbled over the uneven ground. Strips of flesh tingled down the sides of my back. A little more. I clamped my eyes shut, pushing every thought behind me, visualizing the strong white feathers bursting from my skin.

Then, *bang!*

Pain exploded across my chest, blunt and hard, forcing me backward to the ground. I opened my eyes as a red wave of Honeycrisp apples spilled across the grass at my feet. Beyond the mess, the thief glanced back with a sneer. He rounded the last row of tents into the parking lot and hopped into the back of a waiting pickup truck. It sped out of the lot, spitting up dust and gravel, then disappeared down the highway.

I slammed my heel into the ground, sending a small burst of pain through my leg, reminding me of my stupid mortality. Why did humans do such awful things to each other? Free will? More like free pass to be sinful. How could I figure out humanity when it made no sense?

"You should really watch where you're going."

"What?" I shook my head as a strange deep voice and a dark shadow descended over me.

"I said, watch where you're going. That way you won't hurt yourself and bruise all my father's apples." The voice stuck his open hand in my face, and I grabbed on as he hoisted me to my feet in one smooth motion.

"Thanks." I rubbed my hands over my clothes, brushing off the grass and dirt, then looked up. "I was just . . ."

A pair of blue eyes pinned my words to my tongue. Blue like a vast sea on a clear day, the light of the sun reflecting and warming the open air while beneath the surface the currents raged and raced through the fathoms below. A strange balance between tranquil and torrential, drawing me in and threatening to never let me go.

"Trying to run right through me?" He released my hand and took a step back before crouching down to put the pristine red apples I'd knocked to the ground back in their crate. "Hate to tell you, probably not going to work."

Likely not. From the size of his broad shoulders and the soreness that still burned through my torso from the blunt smack, I questioned whether I had actually hit the crate or maybe just banged into his side. I scrambled to the ground to help him pick up the last few strays, trying not to get caught in his stare again. Instead, I focused on his hands. His thick fingers, still holding the last of a summer tan, wrapped delicately around the fruit as he scooped them up.

"No, I was chasing after a thief. If I hadn't run into you, he might not have gotten away."

He settled the last apple in the crate and rested his arm across his thigh. "Thief? What are you talking about?"

"Back there." I pointed toward the far end of the market, my breath still short from the run. "Someone grabbed a bunch of cash from one of the vendors and ran, so I chased him. But then I ran into you and he got away."

He looked over his shoulder, his gaze following my arm, then sprang to his feet scanning the crowd.

I fell back to sit cross-legged on the ground. "Don't worry about it. I already saw them drive away."

"Oh," he sighed, still looking around through the faces. "Then I'm sorry."

"It's not your fault. Unless you're an awful person like that guy. Then maybe it is." I tried to make it a joke, but my sour disdain crept into my tone.

His head tilted to the side as he looked me over, sitting on the ground like a child. "Have we met before?"

"I don't think so. If we did, wouldn't I already know if you were an awful person?" I leaned back and grabbed a runaway apple that had rolled much farther from the rest, then held it up in my palm.

He bent down again and smiled. A light, easy smile that helped to dull my sharp dislike for humans today.

"No, then you would know that I'm definitely not an awful person."

He leaned closer—close enough for me to see how his thick dark hair curled gently behind his ears—and wrapped his hand around the apple. His fingertips grazed my skin and sparks cascaded down my arm, the touch igniting my blood. His eyes widened, maybe feeling it too.

"I'm Griffin. Do you have a name, or is it a secret?" He didn't move, or look away, just kept assessing me with his intense stare.

I cleared my throat. "Yeah, it's—"

"There you are." Chloe's voice boomed as her feet pounded up beside us. She glanced at both our faces then took a step back. "Wait. What happened?"

The spell broke and the world started spinning again. Griffin grabbed the apple and placed it in the crate while I pushed off of the grass and stood.

"Just an accident. Nothing more." I pulled my hands into my sleeves and swung my arms at my sides.

Griffin gave a deep throaty laugh. "You aren't going to tell her that you tried to single-handedly apprehend a thief?"

Chloe's jaw fell open. "You what?"

"Doesn't matter. He got away. But I should probably let the owners know what happened. I just hope they don't think I did it."

"I can tell them if you want," Griffin said. "I know everyone around here. Do you know which stand it was? Or maybe what they sold? That would help."

I closed my eyes and searched my brain. The thief had stood beside a table with yellow containers on it. They had a label. I pressed farther into my memory. Bees. "Honey. They sold honey."

He nodded. "Must be Johnson's Apiary. I'll let them know."

"Griffin, where are those apples?" A middle-aged man appeared around the edge of a bright blue and white tent, his hands on his hips.

"Coming," he shouted back, then grabbed the back of his neck and stared at the ground. "Maybe I'll see you around sometime."

I smiled, the possibility already making my stay here more tolerable. "Maybe."

He hoisted the crate up to his chest, the muscles in his strong arms taut as he rushed toward the tent.

"I left you alone for, like, ten minutes, and you've already chased down a criminal and body checked Griffin Carlisle. Trouble does seem to follow you, doesn't it?" Chloe said, as I kept watching the tent, secretly hoping Griffin would come back.

"Huh?" I blinked and shook my head. "It's not like I'm looking for it. In fact, while I'm here, I want to stay as far away from trouble as I can."

"Then maybe we need to lock you up in the house." She threw an arm over my shoulder. "Did you want to get out of here?"

CHLOE TUGGED my hand and we headed toward the parking lot. Her well-versed knowledge of this Sunday crowd kept me from crashing into more strangers and tumbling to the ground. However, if anyone else looked at me like that Griffin stranger did, I'd welcome it.

So far, I hadn't learned one thing about humanity.

Only how crazy and confusing humans were. The whole planet seemed like a huge mess to me. How would I ever make it an entire week? Hopefully, I could solve Raguel's riddle and I wouldn't have to.

As we neared the border where the grass met the gravel, a strange feeling dragged on the back of my skull. I shook it off, unable to keep up with Chloe's determined pace without full concentration, but the hollowness it left in my stomach became harder to ignore.

The weight pulled again, stronger, deeper into my brain. I turned and scanned the crowd. About twenty feet away a boy stood staring at me, motionless, as everyone else flitted around him. His dirty-blond hair draped over his left eye, but I could still feel his gaze searing through me. When my eyeline crossed his, a smirk curled at the corners of his lips and he raised his left hand, beckoning me closer with his index finger.

I looked away. I'd had enough drama for today. Besides, he'd probably mistaken me for someone else. I didn't know anyone here.

I peeked back over my shoulder, but the broody boy still waited, his laser-sharp focus still targeted on my head. The hollowness in my stomach began to throb, heavy and dark, as the intrigue gnawed at the edges of my thoughts. Maybe I'd dropped something when I crashed into Griffin? Maybe he knew something about the thief? Either way, the only way his insistent stare would likely let go of me was if I answered it.

"Hold on a second, okay?" But I didn't wait for an answer. Instead, I broke my hand from Chloe's and weaved through the shoppers, drawing closer to the stranger like a lost boat following a lighthouse beam to shore.

"Why do you keep staring at me?" I asked once I finally made my way to him. "Can I help you with something?"

"You already have." His sly smile deepened, exposing a glint of white teeth. "I've been looking for you, Arianna."

I crossed my arms, hoping to put some distance between us, already regretting the decision to confront him. His smile grew more sinister, more twisted, and my legs started to tremble. "Are you one of Chloe's friends? How do you know who I am?"

"I know a lot more about you than you think. It's not every day someone falls from the sky like that."

My pulse quickened in my chest and my hands balled into fists. The tremble morphed into a full-out shake. *How did he know?* I glanced around, the dreadful exposed feeling making it hard to breathe. Did anyone else here know my secret?

"I don't know what you're talking about."

"Of course you do." He slid his right hand from his pocket and wrapped my hair around my ear as he leaned closer and whispered, "I wouldn't want people to know either."

"Who are you?"

"Seth. But I have a feeling that's not the question you want to ask, is it?"

"We really better be going." Chloe bounded up beside us and wrapped her arm around my shoulder, tugging me backward and out of Seth's thrall.

A deep breath escaped my throat and I sidled closer to her, never more grateful to see a human before.

"We were just having a conversation. No reason to get jealous." Seth glared at Chloe, but instead of withering at his determination, she planted her hand on her hip and glared right back.

"Not jealous, Seth. We've just got somewhere to be. And that somewhere is far away from you."

"Well then, I guess you'd better go." Seth jutted out his lip in a fake pout then turned back to me. He reached out but I flinched, and he retracted his hand. Smart. Very smart. "But I'm sure I'll see you again."

Chloe swung me around and headed back toward the parking lot. I looked over my shoulder as Seth watched us walk away. I cringed, then focused on the path ahead.

"What was that all about?" I asked, as I struggled to keep up with Chloe's determined steps.

"Nothing. But trust me, if you really want to stay out of trouble, you are definitely going to want to avoid him."

6

The morning sun beat down on the hood of Chloe's Ford Focus and reflected through the windshield. I covered my blinded eyes with my hand and let my head drop down to my chest. High school. Another layer of punishment on top of my already daunting mission. But at least I'd be able to observe. People-watch until maybe something would trigger what I needed to do.

Bang. Bang. Bang.

I jumped as Chloe knocked on the passenger-side window. Her smiling face pressed close to the glass.

"Are you coming?" Her voice sounded muffled and distant, like she was talking from inside a fish bowl.

"Yeah, Chloe." I yawned. "Just a second."

I slowly dragged myself out of the car and shut the door. This human sleep thing didn't make sense. I'd slept all night but felt just as tired this morning. Maybe because my mind wouldn't stop talking. A whole day had passed, and the mystery of humanity still seemed far outside my reach. I'd scanned every face and replayed every interaction, trying to piece together something that might make sense. How would I even know when I was getting close?

When the alarm clock wailed this morning, I had yanked the covers over my head, hoping for a little more rest, or at least a little more clarity. But to keep up with Stephen's rules I would need to at least pretend to go to school.

I tugged at my sweater and adjusted the pretty blue scarf Chloe had lent me. Around us students gathered in groups like polka dots made of people speckled across the school grounds. A few of them stared, sizing me up —a stranger in their territory—but quickly lost interest and looked away. No one seemed to notice I wasn't a typical student, or they simply didn't care. At least I seemed to be blending in.

"C'mon. I don't want to be late for class, and we still need to get your schedule."

"Don't worry about it. I'm sure I can figure it out. Besides, I'll bet it takes time to process someone new."

"Not really. James and Margaret already took care of it. Once we get your schedule, you'll be all set." She smiled in her sweet, helpful way, and I forced a smile back, my stomach churning with the thought of being pinned into a classroom when I had so many other things to do.

We ran up the steps to a set of glass doors and entered a long tiled hallway filled with bodies. Talking. Laughing. Checking themselves over in the mirror. I put my hands over my ears, the noise deafening but also strangely inviting. Chloe grabbed my hand and tugged me down the hall, stopping midway at a wooden door with black lettering that said "Office."

"Just hang on a sec," Chloe said as she disappeared behind the door, leaving me alone in the strange zoo of students.

I grabbed the straps of my backpack and tugged it closer into my chest. Down the hall, the noise erupted as people parted to the side, making way for a group of boys dressed in deep purple and yellow jackets, gold numbers stitched on their left sleeves. I watched them float effortlessly through the crowd, moving in sync. A pack. A unit. An army, marching through the battlefield of high school and commanding its attention.

Toward the front, a familiar face stood out from the rest. Dark wavy hair and bright blue eyes. The apple boy from the farmer's market. Griffin. Number 62.

I tried to shrink into the wall as they passed, not ready to start my day flustered like I'd left him yesterday, but too late. Griffin glanced sideways and noticed me standing near the office door. His eyes caught my stare and he raised his hand with a polite wave, never breaking step with the rest of his group. The skin on my cheeks burned hot, but I waved back and his full lips curled into a smile. A taller guy to his left, number 34, shoved his shoulder into Griffin, knocking him off balance. Griffin simply shrugged, his eyes locked on mine until they'd passed too far and his head couldn't rotate back any farther.

"What was that?" Chloe had emerged from the office, but I hadn't noticed.

A smirk broke across my lips and she shook her head, resting a piece of paper in my hands. I scanned over the grid of subjects and my stomach lurched. Right. I had to go to class.

"What do the purple jackets mean?" I asked as I watched the pack move farther down the hall. A roaring lion patch with its claws bared filled the space between their shoulder blades. "And why does Griffin have one?"

Chloe grimaced and started to walk down the hall. "Football. Those guys are the closest thing to royalty. If the quarterback is the king of high school, then the running back, like Griffin, is the prince. The jacket is just to make sure we all understand. Why? Got a thing for football guys?"

"No. I don't know anything about football. But I'm starting to think I might have a thing for Griffin guys."

"Good luck with that. I've never seen Griffin with anything that resembled a girlfriend."

"Oh, so . . ."

"Who knows? Either way, you've got some fierce competition. He's smart, athletic, has been blessed by the popularity fairy with the gift of amazing genes, and he's one of the least dickish guys on the team. Or at least he's a lot more discreet about it."

"So, is football a big thing here?"

She wrapped her arm over my shoulder. "I don't know what it's like in L.A., but football is kind of a lifestyle out here. You can keep your kale smoothies and avocado toast. We have tailgates and touchdowns."

I wasn't sure I cared much about football but seeing Griffin this morning had me rattled. Maybe it would be worth learning a thing or two?

An irritating bell rang and I shuddered. Chloe

deposited me outside the door of a classroom already
half-filled with students.

"Here's your stop. I'll look for you at lunch."

"Wait. You aren't coming to class?"

"Of course I'm going to class. Chemistry. Down the
hall. We don't have anything together until English
tomorrow."

"Oh." I glanced in the open door and shivered as the
thought of going in on my own slithered up my spine.

Chloe shook her head and nudged my shoulder. "It'll
be fine. Now get in there and try to have a good first
day."

I filed in and headed toward the back, still unsure
why I was continuing with the charade of attending
class. But I needed time to get my thoughts together,
time to think, so getting a few hours uninterrupted with
a notebook and a pen probably wasn't the worst thing
that could happen.

At the back of the classroom I found an empty desk
and slid in, dropping the backpack James and Margaret
had gotten me onto the floor. I undid the zipper and
flipped through the books inside, half hoping there
would be something there to guide me, but instead
found only notebooks with empty pages and a handful
of pens.

"So, you're actually going to pose as one of them?"
Seth had slunk into the desk next to mine and leaned
back in his chair. His smart-ass smirk hadn't disappeared from yesterday, but at least today he'd kept a bit
of distance.

"Can't learn to be human without being human, I
guess." I pulled out a notebook and opened to the first

crisp new page. "Are you going to tell me how you know about . . . well . . . me?"

"Let's just say I know how you feel, being different in their world. Besides, you didn't think you'd be left here without help, did you?"

I dropped my pen on the desk and swiveled to look at Seth directly. "James said I had to do this on my own."

"James and Margaret? Those two old kooks have been in service way too long. Do you honestly think they would know everything planned by the divine?"

Fair point. They had been kind to me, when I probably didn't deserve it, but it didn't mean they actually knew anything more than they needed to.

"So, if you're here to help me, what am I supposed to do? What's my first move?"

"Well—"

"I see you are doing a great job of welcoming our new student, Seth." A teacher with tortoiseshell glasses and wavy silken hair sashayed down the aisle of desks to stop in front of mine. Her lips curled in a smile, but her eyes stabbed sharp as knives. "But may I remind you, this is class time not social hour. And, Seth, you aren't even in this class. Get out."

Seth looked over at me and tipped his head subtly toward the door.

I grabbed my books and began to stand, but the teacher put her hand on my desktop and rapped her knuckles. "I don't think that would be wise. I doubt you want a call home on your first day of class."

"No, ma'am." I dropped back down in the desk and watched Seth's black boots disappear through the classroom door, the hollow slam of it closing in its frame, locking me up tight in my cage.

THE LUNCH BELL rang in time with the fierce growl in my stomach. My morning of sitting on my butt must've taken more energy than I expected. I gathered my things then hurried into the hallway. Chloe was already standing outside the door with a small shopping bag.

"Half a day already down. How do you feel?" she asked, handing me the bag and starting to walk.

I glanced inside. Marvelous food. "Starving."

"Well, good. I packed your lunch. I figured you probably hadn't thought of doing it yourself, and I forgot to warn you that the cafeteria here is dreadful."

"Thanks, but I'd probably eat dirt right now if it stopped the hunger."

She laughed. "Hopefully my sandwiches are a bit better than dirt, but you can let me know."

We walked down the hall and through the side doors of the school. The sun blared down as if it were July instead of late September. Chloe flipped on a pair of green sunglasses and marched out into the heat toward the track and the football field.

"I figured we could eat outside. Grab some sun and just relax."

She pulled out a flannel blanket and spread it on the grass just before the chain-link fence. A few other people had taken their lunches to the bleachers or farther in the back field, soaking up what could be one of the last beautiful warm days of the year.

I sat down beside Chloe and pulled out the many, many options she had provided.

"I didn't know what you liked, so I kind of made one of everything we had."

"Thanks. Now I'll have lunch every day for the rest of the week." If I lasted on Earth that long. Hopefully not.

I ripped open the container with the ham sandwich and tried not to completely devour it in front of her. Knowing her, she might take it as a compliment, but I didn't want to creep her out either.

"So how was your morning?" I asked, trying to make polite conversation as she picked at her own lunch.

"Same old thing. Science. Math. Nothing major. Summer almost blew up her chemistry experiment though. That was kind of entertaining." Her eyes rolled up to the right as she recalled the memory and gave a light giggle. "You should've seen it."

"I'll bet."

A loud buzzing sound came from Chloe's backpack and it started to vibrate on the blanket. I grabbed my sandwich and shuffled away, watching it bounce around, expecting the worst.

"What's that?"

Chloe reached into the front pocket and pulled out a cell phone with a pink and silver houndstooth case. I let out a deep breath.

She slid her thumb around the screen, one hand on her lunch and one hand on her phone. "Just Stacey. She wants to know if I want to go grab an iced cappuccino with her. No big."

She slid the phone back inside her bag and bit down

on her sandwich. A large piece of lettuce pulled out, hitting the side of her face.

"So why don't you go?"

She fixed the lettuce and wiped her face with a napkin. "'Cause I'm here with you. I'm not going to leave you alone on your first day. Unless you want to come with us."

"Not really, but it doesn't mean you can't go. I'll be fine. I kind of wanted to catch my breath before my next class anyway."

Her face brightened, and she placed her palm on my knee. "Really? You wouldn't mind?"

"Of course not."

"Thank you so much. You're the best." She tapped my leg and let out a tiny squeal, then started to pack up her food. "I'll meet you in the parking lot after school, okay?"

I nodded, but I doubt she saw as she hurried away. No sense in making her wait around for me. If all went well, I'd be forgotten by this time next week anyway.

I finished my sandwich, enjoying the peace and quiet and letting my brain wander for a few undisturbed minutes. A warm fall breeze wafted by, taking the burn out of the harsh sun shining bright on the back of my head, my dark chestnut hair drawing it like a magnet. I leaned back, propped up on my elbows, and closed my eyes, savoring the last few minutes left before the deafening bell would ring and I'd be trapped in a box for the next three hours.

A shadow cast over my face. I waited for the cloud to pass, but it never did. One minute. Two minutes. The chill of being away from the sun started to seep into my skin. I opened my eyes and jumped. Seth stood near my extended feet, the sun glowing behind him and blocking out all his features.

I shielded my eyes with my hands. "You again?"

Seth sat down cross-legged beside me on the blanket. He rested his elbows on his knees and steepled his fingers as he leaned in toward me. I inched away slightly, as discreetly as I could. His unexpected presence a little too intense for a casual sunny afternoon.

"Have you made any progress on this mission of yours?"

I sighed and reached into my backpack, pulling out my notebook. "I've been trying to piece things together."

"Whoa. That's a lot of pages. Are you sure you only had two classes this morning?"

"Not funny. There are a lot of pieces to put together, and if I want my wings back, I'm going to have to start solving this puzzle."

He fidgeted with a stack of black and silver rings encircling his thumb, entranced as they spun around and around. "What do you have so far?"

"I don't know." My shoulders deflated inward toward my chest. "What makes people human? I've ripped through everything I could think on biology, psychology, pathology. But I don't think this is going to be some kind of written test. Raguel said he wanted me to experience humanity. Free will. But I don't know what that means."

"Humans are irrational, emotional things. Birth, death, social media likes, love, hate—I think it's all the same to them."

"Wait a minute." I whipped open my notebook to a

fresh page and wrote the word "love" across the top in large loopy letters. "What did you say about love? Maybe that's it."

"You think Raguel sent you here to fall in love? That's kind of insane."

"But why not? He said I needed to experience humanity, and what's more human than love? Up there, everything is unconditional, we are supposed to love Him and His creations, but we don't love each other. That's a human thing. Besides, I asked Raguel for a sign —something to help me when I was at the market—and I think he might have given me one."

Seth fell back onto the blanket, pounding his fist in the grass, howling with laughter. "Right. Like being cast out of Heaven is some new kind of reality dating show. I'm sure there are a lot more important things in this world than love."

"Then why do humans care so much about it? They write stories, compose music, build monuments—all to this one emotion. Maybe that's what he meant about feeling human?"

"You also mentioned free will." Seth sat back up and inched closer on the blanket, a strange look falling over his eyes. "Maybe he wanted you to exercise that. Make some choices. Make some mistakes. Just like the humans do. I'm sure there's a ton of fun things you could do with that free will." He slid his knuckle down the side of my cheek, resting it underneath my chin. He licked his lips, his face moving ever closer. "Don't you want to make your own choices for once?"

My muscles clenched as I pulled my head away. Seth, still moving in, fell forward into my lap.

I pushed him up by his shoulders. "What are you doing?"

He shook his head out, gripping the back of his skull. "Trying to help you have a full human experience. You did ask for my help, didn't you?"

"Yeah, but I think we should leave it at you giving me advice."

He grabbed my hands and wrapped both of his around them. "There's so much more I can show you without using words." He crooked his eyebrow, his hazel eyes swirling with trouble. "Besides, you just said you received a sign from Raguel at the market, and then you met me. I don't think that's a coincidence."

I tugged at my hands, but he held tight. "Let go, Seth."

"I've been on this earth longer than you, and trust me, sometimes being good isn't always the best option."

"I said, let go." I yanked harder and we both tumbled over into the grass.

"Is this guy bothering you?"

I glanced up at Griffin towering over us in his bright purple jacket, four other purple jackets standing in formation behind him.

"No, I think he understands me now." I stretched out my hand, sore from his grasp, and scooted to the far side of the blanket. "Don't you, Seth?"

"Yeah, I understand real well." He glared at Griffin and his army, then at me again. "I should probably be going anyway."

He stood up and straightened his black bomber jacket, giving Griffin a nasty scowl as he pounded off toward the school building.

"You better run, buddy," one of Griffin's friends yelled after him.

Griffin rolled his eyes. "Enough, Alex. Just take the guys out to the field and I'll meet you there."

"Fine, but don't keep us waiting." Alex patted Griffin on the shoulder and gave him a dramatic wink.

Griffin shook his head and rubbed his hand over his face. "Ignore them. They're my best friends, but they can be such losers sometimes."

I stood up, the strange dynamic of him standing over me giving me a weird vibe. "Thanks, but I could've handled it—not that I minded you helping, but just so you know."

"Noted. We were just walking by, and I figured it wouldn't hurt to make sure he got your message."

"Good point. Maybe we'll meet up one day and I won't be a complete disaster."

He chuckled. His light forget-the-world smile broke across his face and erased the icky feeling Seth had branded on my skin.

"But before then, maybe you could tell me your name?"

"Right, I guess I never did. It's Arianna Fell."

He nodded, his eyes turned to the sky as if rolling the words around to see how they felt.

"All right then, Arianna Fell, the girl who can save herself." He started walking toward the field, each step long and slow, then he pointed at me. "Until next time, try to stay out of trouble."

7

"*I*t's decided. I'm going to fall in love with Griffin Carlisle."

"What?" Chloe shook her head like I'd slapped her across the face. She pulled her hands out of the bubbly dishwater in the sink and wiped them on a checkered towel. "You know if you're bored, or need validation or something, you don't need a boyfriend. Why don't you just get a hobby, or a job, or try out for the school play or something?"

"I'm not looking for a boyfriend, silly. I've just never been in love before. And being around Griffin kind of makes my stomach feel all weird, so I figured that would be a good place to start."

"I'm not sure if that's love. Maybe it's just food poisoning?"

"No." I took the stack of dry plates from the counter and hoisted them into the cupboard above my head. "I don't think so."

"Well, what makes him so special then? Besides indigestion?" Chloe scooped her fingers through the bubbles and flicked them at me.

I laughed and wiped my face with the back of my sleeve before snapping the tea towel at her arm. "Well, he's polite. He's been kind to me. Even helped me out with keeping Seth at a distance this afternoon. Plus, look at him. He's like one of the marble statues the ancient Greeks carved. All strong and beautiful and enchanting."

"Okay, I'll give him the fact that he got you to listen to me about Seth, but enchanting? Really?"

"Oh." I stood up straighter, a warm blush growing across my cheeks. "Is he . . . I mean . . . are you already in love with him?"

Her face twisted—her nose, eyes, and lips coming together in a sour scrunch. "Definitely not. He's nice to look at, but after watching that boy suck his thumb in preschool for a year, I don't think I'm ever going to fall in love with him. You have nothing to worry about."

I exhaled. "Good. I wouldn't try to fall in love with someone you were already in love with."

"Well, thank you for thinking of me, but he's all yours."

Chloe pulled the plug in the sink and I stared, entranced, watching the water swirl and empty down the drain.

"The only problem is, you can fall in love with him all you want, but he can just as easily fall in love with someone else."

I stopped and let her logic roll around in my brain. "Good point. I'd better get on it then."

"And what exactly do you plan to do? It's not like you can force these things."

I grabbed a chair at the table and sat down. I'd been devising a plan all afternoon. I wasn't one hundred percent sure how humans worked, but I knew enough to try.

"Okay, so I figure the first thing I need to do is find out more about him."

Chloe leaned on the chair beside me. Her eyes were focused, but her lips were smirking. I couldn't tell if she was interested or amused. "Sounds like a reasonable start."

"To do that, I'll have to find out where he lives, go over to his house, check out his things, maybe watch him for a little bit."

"Okay, stalker. Is that how you ended up getting sent here?"

I frowned. "No, but how else would you get to know someone enough to fall in love with them? Besides, what's a stalker?"

Chloe smacked her forehead with her hand and shook her head. "You, if you go through with this crazy plan. How do you not know what a stalker is?"

"Then what do you suggest I do?"

She tapped her pointer finger against her lips and turned her eyes toward the ceiling. "I'm not quite sure, but I suddenly have a craving for pizza."

"But we just ate."

She walked across the kitchen, slipped her arm around my shoulder, and led me toward the door. "Trust me on this, you're going to love this place. Stacey works there, and it always has just what you are looking for."

"Sure then, I guess."

"Just promise you won't tell people that you are

falling in love with them and that they look 'enchanting'?"

I nodded.

She grabbed her backpack and lifted the car keys from the small rack by the door. "Going to Tony's, Dad," she shouted to Stephen in the living room.

"All right. Don't get into any trouble," he yelled back.

How much trouble could you get in with pizza?

8

*F*at Tony's. An oddly named place for a squat brick building that housed no one I would have defined as fat nor anyone named Tony.

"Come on, let's get a table before it gets busy." Chloe waved her hand and ushered me up the stone stairs to the door. I pushed on the glass and stepped inside, the strange mix of grease and garlic making my mouth water.

"Hey." Stacey met us at the door and pointed at a small table toward the back covered in a red and white checkered plastic tablecloth. I followed Chloe to the table and she dropped her schoolbooks on top.

"What can I get you?" Stacey asked as I took a seat across from Chloe.

"Not much. Just a couple of Cokes for now."

"For sure," she nodded at Chloe and then turned to me. "How are you liking Faraway?"

I shrugged. "Good, I guess."

"You guess? I'm sure it isn't as exciting as L.A. though."

"L.A.? Right, yeah. Definitely not what I'm used to."

"Then you're lucky to have Chloe. She's the best friend anyone could have."

"Seriously, Stacey? I'm not campaigning or anything."

Stacey laughed and tapped her pencil on the edge of the table. "Two Cokes coming up."

"She seems nice." At least now that she didn't think I was a convict.

Chloe opened her blue notebook and flipped to the first empty page. "Yeah, we've known each other since kindergarten. She's the best."

I glanced around the open room, studying the photographs on the walls of hills and rivers. They reminded me of Tuscany and the Tiber, but some were in such bad focus it was hard to tell. Most of the tables were already full, and even though everyone kept their voices down, the noise still bubbled up into a loud din. One of the only few empty tables was a large booth in the corner.

I turned my attention back to Chloe and her open textbook as her hand feverishly scrawled across the notebook page. "What are you working on?"

"Biology. Just have to finish this assignment, and I have a test next week. Sorry if it's boring you."

"No. I was just wondering. If you needed to stay home, we didn't have to come out."

She laughed. "Oh yeah, we did. You'll see." Then she returned to her questions.

I reached into my bag and pulled out my own note-book, skimming all the pages I had written today about what I could do to complete Raguel's mission. If only textbooks existed to teach me that stuff.

Stacey returned with the drinks and placed them on the table with a basket of golden-brown breadsticks.

"Aw. Thanks, Stace," Chloe mumbled as she dropped her pen and grabbed one of the piping hot sticks.

"No problem. Just remember when you're rich and famous that you owe me a favor." Stacey flicked her curly red hair over her shoulder and turned her nose up with a sly smile.

"Absolutely." Chloe bit down on the breadstick and her expression melted, reveling in the taste as she resumed writing in her notebook.

"Do you like biology?" I asked.

She tapped her pen on the edge of her page, then ran the cap down the metal spiral holding the pages together. "Yeah, it's kinda my favorite. But I'm also into chemistry, physics, and calculus. I always hoped to go and get a degree in something like medicine or pharmacy or whatever, but I doubt that's going to happen."

"Why not? If it's something you want to do, then why can't you?"

"Because I doubt I will ever get very far from Faraway."

"But what about free will? If it's something you want, don't you have the choice to go after it?"

Chloe laughed and fell back against her chair. "You're kind of funny, you know that? If everyone got everything they ever wanted, the world would probably implode. Besides, I have other commitments." A darkness crept into the sides of her eyes and she glanced down at her page.

"Maybe. But I think you would make a great doctor one day."

The door swung open, allowing the cool fall breeze to whirl around the room. The swarm of purple and yellow jackets entered one after the other, high fiving, laughing, and generally taking up as much space as they could.

"Do boys always travel in packs like wolves?"

Chloe laughed and glanced over at the door. "Not all of them, but they sure do."

They piled into the open booth in the corner, interrupting everyone's conversations, although it didn't seem like anyone minded. Just when I thought they had finally settled into their spot, the door opened again and Griffin drifted in. Every step seemed to be in slow motion as I watched him swagger toward the corner table, grab a chair, and swing it between his legs, leaning his arms on the back.

"So that's why we're here?" I glared at Chloe and she burst into uncontrollable laughter.

"Maybe. Or maybe we just happened to be here at the same time they happened to be here, which just happens to be after every single Monday night practice?"

"I thought you warned me about being a stalker."

"Technically, you didn't know he'd be here, so I'm the stalker."

"Okay, stalker, what do I do now?"

"Do I have to think of everything? I have no idea. I just got you two in the room. You have to create your own magic."

I buried my face back into my notebook, somehow

wishing the answers to this problem would be something I'd thought of already, but no luck. The voices of the team rumbled throughout the restaurant, or maybe I just imagined that they were louder than the rest, hoping to hear someone mention the weird girl that had practically fallen out of the sky.

"Are you going to just sit there and try not to stare at him all night? Because we could've done that at home."

"Stare at who?" Stacey rested her hand on the back of Chloe's chair and cocked her head to the side.

"This one's got it bad for Griffin Carlisle."

Stacey laughed and smacked her thigh with her hand. "Good luck with that, honey."

"Why does everyone keep saying that?"

"Don't take it the wrong way. I'm just kidding," Stacey said.

"Well, you're probably not far off. I haven't even figured out a way to talk to him, let alone anything else."

"I think your first challenge would be getting him away from the guys for five seconds," Chloe added.

The extra level of difficulty caused my shoulders to slouch, and I slid down in my chair.

"I can help with that," Stacey said. "But I'll probably lose some decent tips for it, so you'd better be ready."

She marched back into the kitchen and I glanced at Chloe. She shrugged and stuck out her bottom lip.

Oh no. Stacey returned to the dining room with her hands full of plastic water glasses. She winked at me as she passed by, and I swiveled in my chair to watch her walk toward the booth. She smiled at the group and started placing glasses in front of the players on the left. She straightened back up, one glass left in her hand, and suddenly it slipped, bouncing twice on the table before splashing all over Griffin.

"I'm so sorry," Stacey said, loud enough for everyone to hear.

Griffin stood and shook out the water from his arms. "Not a big deal," he said and excused himself, heading to the bathroom near the kitchen.

Chloe howled and tossed her head back, while Stacey looked over at us and took a discrete curtsy.

"Stacey is ruthless," Chloe said, putting her hand on her chest to calm her laughter. "Now is your chance, don't waste it."

I stood up and walked toward the bathroom, looking back at Chloe and Stacey who were both silently cheering me on. As I neared the door, the men's room opened, and Griffin rushed out nearly knocking me over.

"Whoa," he said, taking a step back, his hands raised in surrender.

I gasped and tried to act surprised. "It's okay. But I guess we're even now?"

"Yeah, I guess so. Who are you here with?" He shoved his hands deep into his pockets, not in any rush to get away.

"Chloe. We've been doing homework. This seems like a good place to work, and great breadsticks."

He pointed at me. "Your name is Arianna. Right?"

"Yeah." My shoulders dropped. He clearly hadn't been thinking about me the way I had been thinking about him. I was just some girl he had run into, no different than any other day. I should've been grateful he at least remembered my name. My stomach churned, suddenly wanting to be anywhere but here with my clumsy mouth.

"Like, it's Ahr-ianna, not Air-ianna, like air. I've been trying to figure that out."

"Yeah, you're right." He had been thinking about me. He had actually spent more than five minutes of his day thinking about who I was.

He nodded, then glanced over at his friends. "It was good to see you."

I opened my mouth to try and continue the conversation, but he started walking back to his table. I sighed, then retreated to mine, suddenly hating myself for not at least going into the washroom to keep up the charade. As I reached the table, the thought of that conversation being the last time we might talk gnawed at me.

"Griffin," I called after him.

He turned around. "Yeah?"

I sat down at the table with Chloe and waved for him to come over. Surprisingly, he complied and grabbed a chair to sit down between us.

"I forgot to ask you if they ever found the thief from the farmer's market."

His forehead crunched up and a scowl fell across his lips. "No. They think it was probably someone just passing through. No one else noticed the truck, and the police can't do much without a license plate number."

"Oh. I'm really sorry I didn't manage to catch him."

Griffin chuckled. "I don't think you would have anyway. It sounds like they knew what they were doing. Besides," his lips turned up in a shy smile and he looked down toward the table, "if you'd caught the guy, we may have never met."

He leaned closer to me and tapped his thick fingers on the table less than a quarter inch from my hand. A strange feeling built in my stomach, leaving me unsure about whether I wanted to sing from the mountaintops in the low-grade photos of Italy or simply run to the bathroom and throw up. He ran his other hand through his hair then looked down at our nearly touching finger-tips and smiled.

"Aw." Chloe clasped her hands together and batted her eyelashes in a cartoonish way. "That sounds so adorable, Griffin."

He scowled at her, his expression turning from sweet to sour almost instantly.

"It sounds like you guys have a ton to talk about. Maybe you should go do something together sometime, you know, like just the two of you."

Griffin's face blazed red and he stood up from the chair. "I should probably get back." He pointed quickly at his friends and then turned and practically ran across the restaurant.

Chloe watched him walk away, then shrugged. "Well, that could've gone better."

9

*F*all leaves scuttled around my feet as Chloe and I walked into school Tuesday morning. I convinced her to come a little early to avoid the purple parade of Lions and the possibility of locking eyes with Griffin in the hallway. I'd been awake most of the night, running over the awkward rejection I'd received at Tony's and trying to figure out what my next step would be. Love and free will. These were two concepts that should be very simple but were turning out to be a lot more complicated than I had anticipated.

"I just have to run to the library," Chloe said, speeding ahead of me toward the front door, "but I will see you in class."

A happy tingle bubbled through my body as I antici-pated spending time with her in class. It might only be one, but I would take what I could get. I wasn't sure when it had happened, the exact moment when I'd decided I liked this girl-shaped human, but I did. The way her laugh tinkled like silver bells and made me laugh with her. The thoughtful way she took care of the people in her life. The way she cared about me when she didn't have to. I'd only been on Earth three days, but one thing I knew for sure was that being around Chloe Martin made me smile.

The halls were partly filled but not jam-packed like it would be in about fifteen minutes. I rested my forehead against the metal locker and let the coolness wash over me. What was I going to do now? I opened the locker and shoved in my books, then pulled out the timetable and an English text the office had provided. Underneath everything, I glimpsed a white book with gilt-edged pages. I yanked it out and stared at the cover. *The History of Angels.*

Where did this come from? Who else knew my secret? A nervous sensation crept up my back. I looked up and down the hallway, then faced into my locker and opened the book. I flipped through the pages—beautiful painted pictures mixed with columns of text—but there was no indication who it was from.

"See anyone you know?"

I jumped and dropped the book to the floor. It landed with a smack against the tile.

Seth chuckled, then bent over to pick it up and handed it back to me. "Is that any way to treat a gift?"

"What is this for?" I asked, shoving the book deep into the back of my locker.

"So maybe it's not a gift. Maybe it's an apology."

I crossed my arms, the tiny hairs on my skin standing at attention. "Oh."

"I'm really sorry about yesterday. You have no idea how lonely it can be, knowing the things we know and not being able to share them with anyone. I think I just got a little too excited about that."

I closed my locker and sagged against the locker bank. "Don't ever try anything like that again."

"I won't." He backed up a step, clearly understanding the tone of my voice. "I'd rather have you talking to me. Plus, I wouldn't want to get my face bashed in by your blockhead jock boyfriend."

"He's not my boyfriend. I don't think Griffin really wants much to do with me, at least where romance is concerned."

"Oh, well I guess you're going to have to find a new plan then."

"Yes, I guess I am. I'll see you at lunch or something."

I tried to walk away, but Seth kept up with me. "Is there anything that I can do?"

I gave him a sour look.

"Not like that. I mean, maybe I could use some of my contacts to figure out how to get you home."

"You know people who can do that?"

"Maybe. I could ask around, but only if you ask me to."

"Okay. Can you ask around for me, Seth?"

His face lit up and regret clawed at my brain.

"Absolutely. I promise I will make yesterday up to you."

"Not necessary. Just get me out of here."

AFTER SETH LEFT, I crept back to my locker and took the book out again. I ran my right hand over the beautiful embossed cover. The gift was actually quite thoughtful, but something about Seth tainted it. I wanted to trust him, but he always came off as too aggressive. If he really wanted to help, he needed to tone it down.

I slipped into English class early and flipped through the pages of the book, hoping for something to make sense. Unfortunately, most of the text seemed to be descriptions of the angels instead of anything useful. I stopped on a page near the middle. A familiar set of blue robes and gilded wings flowed across two full pages. "Raguel, Angel of Justice" it said in the corner. I traced my finger over his long silver hair. *Why can't you just tell me what I need to do?*

"Thanks for saving me a seat." Chloe dropped her bag on the desk next to mine.

I slammed the book closed and shoved it into my backpack. "Hey, did you get what you needed at the library?"

"Yup." She picked a book out of her bag and shook it in front of me, then put it back and took her seat. "Did I see you talking to that Seth guy in the hallway?"

I nodded.

"He kind of creeps me out, but you can do what you want, I guess. What did you call it? 'Free will' and all?"

The first bell squawked, and the room started to fill with students. The English teacher, Mr. Richter, followed behind with a worn leather shoulder bag and a navy sport coat.

"Seats, students. The challenge to expand your young

minds in only an hour is already daunting. Don't waste an extra minute."

He dropped the bag onto his desk and smiled at everyone.

"Let's get down to business, shall we? I'm going to need everybody to grab a partner for this next assignment. You have two minutes," he flipped his wrist toward his face and tapped the top of his watch with his fingernail, "and go."

Immediately Chloe and I turned to each other and yelled in unison, "Partners?"

"Of course." I grinned and watched as everyone else scrambled around the room, searching for the perfect partner, not wanting to be left out. Fortunately, math had blessed them, as the class held an even number of students.

"And time," Mr. Richter said as he walked across the front of the classroom, tugged the thighs of his pants up slightly, and sat on the edge of his desk. "You are going to be interviewing your partner and turning in the transcript to me next Tuesday. All you kids with your social media—all that snap-chatty-twitter-insta somethings—we have lost the art of true conversation. Plus, it is vitally important that you know how to pose questions and answer them properly for when you interview for the soul-sucking jobs that you will all have one day."

A girl in the middle of the room shot her hand into the air.

"Yes, Abigail," Mr. Richter said, waving his hand toward her.

"Do we all have the same questions, or will they be different?"

"Well, that's where the fun part begins. You will be brainstorming the questions to ask your partner. I understand for some it may be more of a light drizzle than a full storm, but I expect everyone to come up with at least twenty questions that can be answered without a simple yes or no. Grading will be based on the quality of the questions asked as well as the quality of the answers you provide your partner."

The classroom door opened and clicked quietly shut as Griffin slipped through the door. I slid down in my desk and rubbed my hand over my face.

Griffin's stealth skills were no match for the hawk-like instructor in charge. "Mr. Carlisle, it is a pleasure for you to join us today."

He glanced down at the floor, his breath short. "I'm sorry. Coach needed to talk to me."

"Well, I will be having a chat with Coach Beaufort. His time with you is precious, but so is mine. We have already found partners for our new assignment, Mr. Carlisle, so you will need to catch up as I do not like to repeat myself."

Alex waved his purple arm in the air for Griffin to take the empty seat next to him and one of the other guys from the team. He nodded in their direction and headed toward that end of the classroom.

"Oh, no, Mr. Carlisle. As you have chosen to be tardy and everyone else has already been paired off success-fully, I will be choosing your group for you." He scanned the classroom and clasped his hands together when he spied the empty chair beside Chloe. "You'll be joining Ms. Martin and Ms. Fell. Ladies, hopefully you can teach

Mr. Carlisle a thing or two." He looked back at Griffin. "Pray they take mercy on you."

Griffin collapsed into the empty desk. His eyes traveled from Chloe to me, and a sheepish grin broke across his face. "Hey."

10

"*C*hloe, coming here was pure genius." I took a deep swig of my iced tea and another bite of breadstick. The buttery, garlicky, cheesy taste jumbled in my mouth into a mush of utter joy on my tongue.

"Easy, now. Don't want you falling into a carb coma before we finish this assignment." Chloe grabbed the empty bread basket and placed it on the side of the circular booth. "Isn't it much better doing this here than at our place with my dad standing over us?"

"Or mine," Griffin added with his eyebrows raised and a nasty snarl.

I swallowed, watching his odd expression. I'd only known him a few days, but I'd never seen him truly angry. Even when he'd stared down Seth near the bleachers, the emotions never reached his deep blue eyes. But tonight, the seas were stormy, bashing ships along the shoreline.

"Okay, who's turn is it?"

Both Griffin and Chloe shrugged. As a duo, this assignment could have been a simple back-and-forth interview, but as a triad Mr. Richter had insisted we split the questions, each asking our other partners ten, but we kept talking between the answers and always seemed to lose our place.

"Maybe it's mine?" Griffin took the back of his pen and counted silently down the page, alternating our names until he hit the bottom.

I took the opportunity to watch him. His dark red lips moving slowly as he whispered. The way he clenched his jaw as his mind processed. The slight curl at the tips of his eyelashes as he blinked from staring at his notes. Each piece of him fit together like a stunning puzzle that I wanted to spend hours trying to solve. There was only one missing piece.

I still didn't understand why he'd been so awkward the other night. He'd barely spoken in class, but now, here, under the cheap stained-glass imitation Tiffanies, he'd opened up again. Been the confident and intoxicating apple boy I'd met at the farmer's market.

"Ari, it's your turn to ask Chloe."

Chloe wrinkled her nose. "Ew. Why do you insist on calling her that?"

"Why not?" He shrugged and turned to me, studying my face. "You don't mind, do you?"

"Not really. But I've never had anyone call me anything other than my full name before."

"Because your full name is beautiful. Don't let him shorten it just because he's too lazy to say three full syllables."

Griffin snickered and shook his head. "Judge much, Chlo."

Chloe cringed and gripped her pen tight in her fist.

"It's not 'cause I'm lazy. I give lots of people nicknames. I never call any of my friends by their full first names. Dozer. Ry. Chuckie. Bronx."

"That sounds like you're listing dwarves, Snow White. Besides, what about Alex? He's your best friend, isn't he?" She crossed her arms and waggled her head with a smug look.

"Alex, short for Alexander." Griffin picked up a straw wrapper and tossed it into the hoop of her arms like a basketball, then cheered, his arms in the air, when it landed right in the middle.

"So, it's a compliment then?" I asked, making sure I'd heard correctly. Or maybe just wanting to hear him say it again.

"Yep. Unless you'd rather I didn't?"

He slid closer to me on the bench, the calm, still water returning to his gaze and holding me there to drift. The heat of his skin rolled off him and landed on my arms. I held my breath for a second, enjoying the sensation and letting the world float away, but then I shook my head and grabbed my notebook.

"Okay, Chloe, what is your greatest weakness?"

She chewed on the top of her pen for a few seconds, staring at the ceiling. "Hmmm, weakness?"

"Well, your insult game is weak." Griffin snickered at her.

She rolled her eyes and dropped the pen on the table. "I have to say, I take things too personally sometimes."

"Fair answer. I'd agree." Griffin nodded.

"I wasn't telling you." She looked down at her notes. "Question twenty, what was the real reason you were late for class yesterday, Griffin?"

"Let me see that." He reached across the table and grabbed her notebook as she smirked in the corner. "You can't ask me that. You know what Richter would do to me."

Chloe took a drink, using the straw to hide her mischievous smile. "Maybe not. But I know Coach Beaufort has an early morning Pilates class at the Faraway Community Center on Tuesday mornings, so he was definitely not talking to you."

Griffin looked away, staring out the window to the street, red creeping up the sides of his face. "I had a fight with my dad, and I was late."

I caught his lost stare. "Why didn't you just tell Mr. Richter that?"

"Nobody really needs to know. Plus, I doubt it would've mattered. He would have made me twist like a worm on a hook no matter what I said."

"But maybe he would've put you in a different group."

"What's the matter? Don't like your group?"

Chloe stuck out her lower lip and chuckled. "Could be better."

"All right, Griffin," I asked, trying to put the evening back in order. "What are your plans after high school?"

"To get as far away from here as possible."

"Great answer, scholar."

"There's more, Chloe. I'm still hoping that I can pull

a football scholarship, but I really want to go to school where it's warm. Florida, California, Texas, something like that. Then I want to get a degree in something help-ful, like law or veterinary science."

I clapped my hands quickly and clasped them together. "Oh. Chloe loves science. She says she wants to be a doctor someday."

"Really? Where are you applying?"

Chloe glared at me through narrowed eyes, her lips a stern line. "Nowhere. I doubt I'm going to be going to college."

Griffin and I looked at each other, both our mouths open but with no words flowing out. Like when the tele-vision has the sound turned down.

Eventually, Griffin broke the silence. "You're from L.A., right, Ari?"

I nodded. It sounded like the right place. I really needed to write these things down.

He shifted in the booth, bringing his knee up and his shoulders square to me. "Do you plan on going back there? If I end up at a California school, maybe we can meet up some time and you can show me around? It'd be really great to have someone there who knows the place—"

"Can we please stop talking about college?" Chloe's sarcastic tone had faded, and this time she wasn't joking around.

"Why? Everyone is going to be talking about it sooner or later. You might want to stay here, but almost everyone else will be leaving."

"Yep," Chloe whispered. "Everybody always leaves."

"Okay, another question." Griffin scanned the list of questions, clearly looking for something neutral, skipping over ones I knew he hadn't asked yet. "Here's a good one, Ari—"

"I'm done mine, so I think I'm just going to go." Chloe stood and shoved her books in her bag, her eyes darting back and forth. She put her hand on her forehead. "Where is my pen? Has anyone seen my pen?"

"It's right here on the table." I picked up the chewed blue Bic and held it up.

"Thanks." She shoved it in the bag, glassy tears building as her breathing shortened.

"Are you okay, Chloe?" Griffin asked.

"Yep. I'm fine. You guys stay here, finish your stuff." She started to walk away, then stopped and clenched her fist in the air. She retreated backward to the table. "Griffin, could you please drive Arianna home?"

He glanced over at me with a questioning stare. "Sure."

"Great. Perfect."

Chloe sped out the door, tossing her backpack over her shoulder and nearly taking out the plastic plant near the front door.

I shook my head. "Wait." I stacked my books in a haphazard pile and tried to stand, the booth keeping my legs partially bent. "I'd better go after her."

Griffin grabbed my hand. "Are you sure you can't stay? She said she'd be fine."

I glanced down at my hand in his, his thumb drawing lines up and down my fingers. I sighed. "I know, but I have a feeling she's not."

I slid out of the booth, watching the disappointment creep across his face. He actually wanted me to stay. I stopped, curling my hand into a fist and knocking it on the table, but my eyes kept watching out the window, knowing my feet should be following her out the door. I glanced back at Griffin. Sweet, handsome Griffin. But he'd have to wait.

I pushed open the door as Chloe's taillights rounded the corner.

Shoot.

I smacked my fist on the stone railing. Why didn't I just follow my gut in the first place? At least I only had to walk a few blocks.

"Hey." Seth stood a little way down the sidewalk, leaning against a lamppost. His arms were crossed and one leg was pulled up with his sole flat against the metal —kind of like a flamingo with an attitude. He peeled himself from his perch and walked to the bottom of the restaurant's steps, holding each of the handrails and blocking my exit.

"Hey." I raced down the stairs, hoping he would get the hint and move aside, but he simply hung on tighter, swinging back slightly to give me a little more space but not setting me free.

"How's the study group?"

"Over. But I really need to get going."

He swung back, releasing his arm, and I bolted for the opening between him and the railing, but he rebounded, closing the gap before I could get through.

"Okay, but I came here to warn you."

"About what, Seth? I really have to go."

"I've been hearing things. Rumblings that certain

groups have figured out that you're here. Certain groups that would love to get ahold of someone like you to prove a point."

"Prove a point? To who?"

The playful expression drained from his face, replaced by dark reflections of shade and shadow. His hands gripped the rail tighter, his knuckles glowing white under the streetlamp.

"I don't think you realize, there is a much bigger game going on here. Good versus evil. Above against below. Each side needs soldiers, and you are standing on middle ground, ripe for recruitment. This war will span the centuries, but every single battle counts."

"So, what exactly are you trying to say? Who am I running from?" I crossed my arms and leaned against the handrail, knowing I wouldn't be getting through until Seth had said his piece or I dropped my shoulder and took him out of my way. But something told me it would not be that simple, so I'd have to wait him out.

"I'm not sure, but you should definitely watch your back. And I would suggest that you stop wasting time with the humans. The longer you're on Earth as an angel, the bigger the threat becomes."

"Understood. But right now, I really need to get back home."

"That's what I'm saying. You need to go home. Let me help you."

"No, that's not what I meant. Chloe's. I need to go to Chloe's house."

He pushed off the rails, finally standing back to let me pass. "Maybe I should walk you back, just in case something happens."

"No, it's just a few blocks. I'll be fine. But thank you, Seth." I rested my hand on his chest for a moment and gave it a quick pat before turning and heading down the sidewalk.

"Remember what I said, Arianna. Be careful."

11

I burst into the house. The hollow sound of the door closing echoed through the quiet rooms. Quiet, except for Stephen snoring in front of the television. I crept on my tiptoes down the hall. Chloe's room sat empty, even though I'd seen her car parked in the driveway. I checked my room, the bathroom, the basement, but couldn't find her.

I headed back into the kitchen and leaned against the counter. My breathing was hard and labored after running all the way from Tony's and scouring the house. I poured myself a glass of water then noticed a small light glowing on the deck through the patio door. I set the water down on the counter and peeked through the glass door pane. Chloe sat wrapped in a blanket in a large wooden chair, staring up at the sky.

I slid the door open and sat in the chair across from her. She didn't bother to look up or even acknowledge my interruption. Glistening streams flowed from her eyes to her chin, but she didn't seem to be crying anymore. Possibly she'd already cried everything out.

"You ever just sit and look at the stars and wonder if there's even anything up there?" she asked finally, her voice small and far away.

"Not really. They just seem so tiny—not like they're supposed to be. Stars are meant to be these huge magnificent things, but from down here all we see are specks."

"Yeah, I guess you're right." She let out a heavy sigh and settled farther back in her chair, pulling the blanket tighter around her chest.

"What happened back there?"

"I just . . . I just started thinking about my mom, and I didn't want to be a downer for you and Griffin."

"Don't worry about us. I was worried about you. What happened anyway?" I leaned forward in my chair, bridging the gap between us, but she continued to stare at the sky.

"Cancer. Just over two years now. By the time they found out, it had already taken over most of her body. It was only about six months in and out of the hospital before she was gone."

"I'm sorry. Is that why you ran off? You miss her?"

"No, I just felt guilty again."

"Guilty?"

"Yeah. All I remember is that after she died, I was so mad at her. I hated her for leaving me. Hated myself for thinking it."

"I'm sure she would understand. It isn't easy when you lose someone. There isn't a right way to react."

"Maybe." She raised her arm from under the blanket

and wiped her eyes, catching a stray tear on the tip of her index finger and flicking it to the ground. "But every time I think of her, all I think about is how much I regret being angry."

"You really think she'd want you to feel that way if she were here?"

"No. But I doubt a lot of things would be the way they are if she were here."

I put my elbows on my knees and hooked my fingers together, pulling them apart and rehooking them over and over, not knowing how far I could go. Knowing I'd probably overstep anyway. "Like you going away to college instead of staying home to take care of your father."

"Something like that."

"Did he ever tell you to stay?"

"No. And he never would. I just don't know how he would be on his own. He misses her so much every day. She was everything to him. To us."

"But sometimes, maybe, you have to let go a bit."

She shifted in her place then took a drink of water from the glass resting on the deck. She looked at the sky again, but her eyes seemed to be staring beyond the stars. Somewhere they couldn't reach. I sat back and looked up too, hoping to find the magic she seemed to think was there.

"Is that why you're here? Are you just letting go of something?"

"No. I saw somebody make a bad choice. Choosing to put themselves in danger and risking the ones they loved, and I couldn't stand it, so I got in the way."

"That doesn't sound like such a bad thing."

"It is, when you've been told not to. Everybody has the right to make their own choices, and I didn't honor that."

"Well don't you have the right to stop them? I mean, if they continue to do the wrong thing, can't you choose to do the right thing and make it better?"

"Yeah. I wish that was true. But then I wouldn't have gotten to come here and meet you." I forced a smile and put my hand on her arm. She smiled back with the same amount of enthusiasm.

"Already stealing Griffin's cheesy lines. Maybe you are meant to be together. I hope I didn't mess things up for you back there. He seems to really like you."

"Yeah. And I'm really starting to like him. But it's not a line. I like you too, and I don't like to see you hurting."

"Thanks. I might get used to having you around here. Do you know how long you're going to stay yet?"

My mind raced for an answer, but instead of the truth—that I likely wouldn't last the week—I slipped out, "Not too sure yet."

"Well, I hope you get to stay for a while."

I patted her arm, stroking the soft blanket, warmth building under my palm.

"Me too."

12

I dropped my backpack on the school desk and rested my head on the makeshift pillow of lumpy books inside. My entire body hung limp, exhausted from lack of sleep, but I didn't care. I'd stayed out with Chloe until the chilling fall air seeped deep into our bones and made it too uncomfortable to sit on the deck. Then we'd simply moved inside, talking and laughing late into the night until we both fell asleep. Now, the only thing left to bother me was the nagging feeling at the back of my brain that in a few days I'd have to leave her.

"Well, you look like hell." Seth dropped into the desk beside me, effortless and uncouth as usual. "What happened?"

"Nothing. Just didn't get much sleep last night."

He raised his left eyebrow into an arch and stared at me.

"Nothing, Seth. Nothing for you to be concerned about anyway."

"Good. I didn't want to lose my breakfast over you gushing about that purple-coated knucklehead."

I wrinkled my nose at the insult, but Griffin and Seth were as far apart as two beings could be, so how did I expect him to understand? Besides, I didn't have the energy to argue with him.

"But I did want to talk about our conversation last night. I've heard—"

"Seth, I appreciate your attempts to make new friends, but again, you aren't in this class." Mrs. Walker, the bespectacled math teacher, said as she darted down the row of desks and loomed over ours.

"Yes, Mrs. Walker."

"Save your socializing for break, or post about it online or something for Miss Fell to read later." She flitted her hand in the air.

Seth winked and slipped out of the desk, heading toward the door. Mrs. Walker stood over me and cleared her throat until I opened my backpack and pulled out a notebook. Then she turned and headed back toward the front of the class.

"All right, everyone. As I was discussing on Monday if x is the square root of m—"

A hissing crackle came from the speaker in the corner of the room. "Could Arianna Fell please report to the principal's office? Arianna Fell to the principal's office."

Mrs. Walker looked at me then nodded, swiping her hand through the air toward the door. I grabbed my backpack and slipped out into the nearly empty hallway.

I entered the office. Three students sat lined up in chairs along the wall, one with a bleeding nose and another at the other end nursing a swollen fist. The secretary behind the desk, Ms. Collins as the nameplate near her coffee cup read, ignored the students, her fingers flitting across her keyboard as her lacquered nails clacked on the keys, eyes glued to the screen.

"Hello, I just got called down to the off—"

She whipped a piece of paper in the air between her index and pointer finger, her eyes still intent on the computer monitor. "A message for you."

"Thank you." I hesitated for a moment, then took the note from her hands.

Welcome to Faraway High School.

Please report immediately to the music room for new student orientation.

A LITTLE LATE, but at least it got me out of math class.

"Excuse me, can you tell me where the music room is?" I asked the secretary.

"Down the hall, up the stairs to the second floor, then down at the end of that hallway take the stairs on your left."

The kid with the bleeding nose glared at the kid with the broken fist, while the guy in the middle tried to keep his distance from either side. I rushed out of the office and followed the directions to likely the farthest point in the school, except for maybe the ends of the soccer field out back.

I opened the door, but other than the instruments the room was empty. I pulled the note out of my pocket and read it again. There was no time on it and no date, so maybe I had missed it. Maybe I should have received this note two days ago when I'd actually been new. Either way, the delightful silence drew me deeper inside.

The design of this room didn't match the other class-rooms in the school. It looked more like a lecture hall with carpeted risers ascending in a theater-type forma-tion. I walked farther in, running my hands along the tops of the plastic chairs and music stands as I ascended the row of stairs. In the far corner I tapped my hands on the bass drum, reveling in the hollow sound that rever-berated in the empty room. I closed my eyes, feeling the sound, then enjoying the silence as the noise hushed and died.

"Arianna Fell?"

I jumped at the voice. A tall, lanky guy walked into the room, closing the door behind him. He didn't look familiar—his fascinating, wild curly hair would've stuck in my memory—but something put me on edge. I'd felt this feeling before. This sick, gnawing feeling in my gut.

"Yes, that's me."

"Perfect. I'm so glad you could meet me here." He started walking up the far side of the room toward the top.

"So, the note said this is new student orientation?"

"Not quite. Clever name, though. Arianna Fell." He chuckled, but the sound seemed darker. Menacing. "You come up with that? I love the whole hiding-in-plain-sight vibe it has."

"What do you mean?" The weight of my body slid to

my toes as the ominous laugh of the stranger reverberated through the acoustics in the room.

"You know . . ." He raised his hand in the air, his two fingers mimicking legs dropping down and smashing into the palm of his other hand while he made a high-pitched whistling noise. "You're a fallen, so you fell."

"Are you friends with Seth?"

"Seth?" He tapped his finger on his chin and rolled his eyes toward the ceiling. "Doesn't ring a bell. But then again, I don't have a lot of friends." He slipped off his glasses and slid them into the back pocket of his jeans. "So, is this your true form? I mean, if I just tack on a pair of fluffy wings and a halo, would this be how you look all the time?"

I nodded, my eyes flashing between him and the door. I slowly inched my way to the end of the stairs, trying not to alert him, crafting a plan to eliminate the line of chairs in my way.

"Well they sure do make them pretty in Heaven, don't they, Arianna?"

I stepped back again. *Crash!* A set of chimes tumbled to the floor, making a tinkling smash as they clanked together on the floor. My pulse pounded hard against my pressure points.

"Demons aren't quite as pleasing to the eye, but we do okay. Did you want to see my true form?"

"No, I'm okay."

He stepped toward me, moving faster, and I slid one of the chairs out of the way and moved down the steps.

"I should probably get back to class."

"Not yet. We were just about to have a little fun."

I threw my hand in front of me. "Come any closer and I'll scream."

"Scream all you want. This is a soundproof room in the farthest corner of the building. Do you actually think I would be that stupid?" He laughed, tossing his head back, the seams of his soul coming undone. "Now for a proper introduction."

He hooked his pointer finger to the inside of his cheek and pulled, stretching his devious smile. The rest of his face blurred and shifted until none of his human face remained. His hair stood on end, morphing into two gnarled black horns extending from the top of his greenish-yellow scalp. Glowing crimson orbs seared through his eye sockets. A row of jagged, sharp teeth protruded from his bottom jaw over the top of his dark black lips.

My pulse hammered at my temples. "What do you want?"

He snorted, his head facing the ceiling. "One less angel on Team Heaven."

13

I chucked the chairs out of the way, racing toward the front of the classroom and the one and only exit. Behind me the demon cackled, trampling through the rows, his voice echoing closer and closer. I grabbed one of the music stands and threw it at him. His arm swiped through the air, knocking it aside like a toothpick. I raced forward, pushing myself as fast as I could go, ripping chairs and stands and instruments behind me. I needed wings. I needed something. This human body wouldn't withstand five minutes with a demon.

As I crested the last stair, a clawed hand grabbed my shoulder. I dropped to the ground, crawling on my elbows, trying to get my feet back under me. The demon's hand grabbed my ankle. I steadied on one arm and kicked with my free foot, connecting with the beast's jaw. It yowled and I wrenched my foot from its grip. Pushing up quickly, I made it the last few feet to the door. I turned the knob. The cool breeze of freedom wafted in through the slight crack.

My head wrenched backward. The demon sank its claws deep into my hair and pulled, dragging me back into the room, my roots screaming with pain against my scalp. He pushed me against the wall, his claws still tangled in the ends of my tresses.

"Not so powerful without your wings, huh, angel?"

I twisted in his grip, but he held my head firmly against the wall. "Please don't hurt me. Maybe there is something else I can do for you. Maybe you don't have to hurt me."

The demon laughed. His breath stank of cigarette butts mixed with turpentine. But I held strong, hoping anything could be more important than seeing me dead.

"But where's the fun in that?"

I kicked and punched as hard as I could, my fists no match against his concrete wall of a chest. He laughed louder, pressing my body harder against the wall until I could no longer move. I closed my eyes, wondering if Raguel would take me back if I died.

The door burst open. Seth rushed in and slammed into the demon, knocking him to the ground.

"Leave her alone," he yelled, his eyes flitting from me to the demon and back again.

"Why? She'll only be trouble. Consider this a favor."

Seth's hands became fists. The top of his head lowered as his entire body vibrated, red spouting up from his neck. He threw his hand out in front of him and light sparked from his palm straight into the demon's torso. The demon screamed, as if Seth were ripping the skin from his body.

"Don't ever let me see you back here again," Seth shouted. The veins near his temples throbbed as all the force in his body funneled out through his hand. The caustic smell of burnt hair and rubber filled the room and I gagged, clamping my hand over my mouth and turning my eyes away as the demon writhed upon the floor.

Finally, Seth's light faded. He stumbled back a few steps, grabbing hold of the desk at the front of the room to keep from falling over. I rushed toward him to help him stand. His arms fell onto my shoulders, gripping me tightly with shaking fingers.

"What just happened?" I asked, wrapping an arm around his waist trying to keep him upright.

Seth shook his head, blinking his eyes several times. "I heard your name when you were called to the office. You never made it back to your class, so I came looking for you. Good thing I showed when I did."

I glanced back at the small charred spot on the floor where the demon's body used to be. "Yeah. It is. I don't know how he found me."

"I told you that people were starting to talk. I guess this guy wasn't willing to wait to see if the rumors were true."

"Well, thank you, Seth. If you'd been a few minutes later, I don't know what would've happened." I leaned closer into him, giving him a hug and resting my head on his shoulder. He wrapped his arms around me, hesitant at first, then slowly pulling me tighter. The murky smell of burning wood rolled off his skin. My breath hitched in my throat and tears pooled in my eyes, the last bits of adrenaline wearing off and letting the gravity of the threat sink into my flesh.

"Hey, it's okay." Seth rested his chin on the top of my head. "He's gone and I doubt he'll be back."

"How come you have powers here? I am totally defenseless, but you have the chance to save yourself."

"Just lucky, I guess."

"Thank you. And I think you're right. I can't keep wasting time. I need to finish this and get back home."

He slid his hands up around my biceps and pushed me back so he could see my face. "I'm here to help you. Anything you need."

The grating sound of the bell went off and I twitched under Seth's hands.

"And if you trust me, I have an idea about what you can do to speed things up. I know someone, if you just choose to see them."

I shook my head. "Not yet. I don't want to leave this in anyone else's hands. If I'm going to complete Raguel's task, I know what I need to do."

Seth's eyes widened, and he licked his lips patiently, hanging on what I might say.

"Thank you, Seth, but I have to go. I'll explain later."

I exited the room and ran down the stairs into the slowly filling second floor hallway. I held my breath and rushed between the students until I reached the main staircase, taking the steps two at a time to the main floor.

I scanned the crowd until I saw the familiar spot of purple looming in the middle near the locker bank.

Marching straight into the Lion's den, I tapped Griffin on the shoulder. He spun around, his jaw dropping and recovering into a warm smile, then melting into a frown of concern.

"Ari, are you okay? You're shaking."

I glanced down at my trembling hands and the ripped legging near my ankle. Hopefully I just looked afraid—no blood or any other markings I'd have to explain.

"Yeah. Having a bad day. But I need to say something."

He slid out of the pack, guarding me from them with his broad shoulders. "What's wrong?"

"I don't want to wait around anymore. Did you want to do something with me? Away from here, without everyone else?"

He grabbed the back of his neck and stared down at the floor. "Did you just ask me out?"

His voice caught the attention of the rest of his teammates, and they began hooting and whistling behind his back. Pink tinged the top of his cheeks, his eyes averted from mine.

"Yeah, I think I did. So?"

"I . . . I don't think that's a good idea."

"Oh." It was the only word I could think to say as my stomach hollowed and the hallway started to spin. "I just thought . . . but I guess . . . never mind."

I spun around and sped away as fast as I could. A run-in with a demon and now this. I'd never make it back home.

I raced to my locker, determined to bury my head in the middle of the black metal hole. Ahead of me Seth stood at the end of the stairs, shaking his head, but I didn't care to hear about his disappointment. It didn't matter anyway.

A hand fell on my shoulder and I whirled around. "What?"

Griffin took a step back at my snap.

"I changed my mind. I don't know what it is about you, but I think I need to find out."

I exhaled, letting the pent-up anger drift out of my body—or at least some of it.

"Perfect. Tonight?"

His eyes bulged, then he shifted his weight between his feet. "Can't. I have practice. Tomorrow? Tomorrow would be good."

"Okay. Are you sure?"

"No. But I haven't been sure about anything since you tried to tackle me last Sunday." He smiled and my lips turned up as well.

"Okay. Tomorrow. I can meet you at your place."

His face hardened, stone cold and steel gray. "Better not. I'll come get you."

"Sure. But only because I really don't know where you live."

He shook his head, laughing to himself, and walked off down the hallway. I turned back to see Seth, his stare terrifying me to my core. I shrugged, but he didn't respond. He simply turned and walked away.

14

"*D*id you hear that someone trashed the music room today?"

I coughed on the bite of spaghetti in my mouth, the shock sending the noodles the wrong way down my throat. I gulped down half my water glass and forced myself to breathe.

"No. Really? Do they know who did it?" I pushed a meatball around my plate, waiting for her to drop the bomb.

"Not sure. All I heard was that a bunch of chairs and stands were thrown around, and there was an odd burn mark on the carpet."

My body relaxed and I melted into my seat. "Burn mark? That seems weird."

"Yeah, right? Maybe someone was smoking or something in there or tried to burn down the school and got caught. I don't know."

"That school seems to be getting rougher all the

time." Stephen took a big bite of food and shook his head.

"Did you want to send me to the other high school in the town that only has one high school?" Chloe laughed.

"You're just lucky it isn't you getting into trouble." His eyebrows came together and his eyes narrowed, but the smile sprawled across his lips gave him away.

"I wonder if that Seth guy was involved," Chloe said, twirling the noodles on her fork like a pro, then shoving them into her mouth.

I shrugged. "Why would you think that? He's a bit intense, but I don't think he's that bad."

"Now hold on a second. I hope Chloe's been helping you make some decent friends here. This Seth guy isn't going to be a problem, is he?" Stephen's playful tone vanished, his concern pouring out of his eyes, straight at me.

Chloe waved her empty fork in the air. "Relax, Dad. Arianna is fine. No reason to panic." Then she pointed her fork in my direction and narrowed her stare. "But to answer your question, you might think Seth just seems intense, but whenever something bad happens around here, he's usually somewhere close by. It's like all the mysterious bad things converge into one hurricane Seth." She nodded, seemingly satisfied with diffusing the situation, and resumed spinning her spaghetti noodles on her plate. Without looking up, she continued. "Besides, Dad, you can chill. Arianna is dating Griffin Carlisle."

The worry creases in his brow ironed flat. "Ah, Griffin. Nice kid. Been having a rough year though. Not a lot of points up on that scoreboard."

"Arianna doesn't really care much for football."

Stephen stood. "Well then you're going to have to get out of my house." He pointed at the door.

My hands began to shake, and I dropped my fork to my plate. "Oh. Maybe I could try . . ." I stammered, but Chloe reached over and grabbed my hand.

"He's just kidding. Remember, football is life. I thought I warned you of that already."

"Right." I picked up my fork again, heat building at the tops of my ears.

"How did you hear about me and Griffin?"

"How did I not hear? The whole school is talking about it. It's the first time anyone's ever seen a girl that much on a mission for a date. And the fact that he said yes is just blowing people's minds. I'm just mad you hadn't told me yet."

"I planned to, I just hadn't found the right way to mention it yet. Did I do this wrong?"

"No. I think it was awesome. And besides, maybe if things go well, he'll ask you to the homecoming dance."

"Homecoming dance?"

"Okay, sometimes I swear you're from another planet. The homecoming dance. The posters all over everywhere."

"I haven't been here that long. I guess I never noticed. Are you going?"

"Yeah. Brad is taking me."

"Oh, I didn't realize that you and Brad . . ."

"Yeah, I don't know if there is a me and Brad, but I guess maybe we'll see?" She raised her eyebrows and waggled them at me.

Stephen put his hands over his ears. "I don't know if I

want to hear this. I am pretty sure I don't want to hear this. La la la." He stood up and grabbed his empty plate while keeping one hand over his right ear, then dumped the plate into the sink. "I think I'm going to go see if there is a game on."

"Sure, Dad. We can wait for you to come back to talk about boys."

"I can't hear you," he said as he neared the hall.

"Dad," Chloe's voice dropped, the humor vanishing, "did you take your pills today?"

"Of course," he said. He doubled back toward his daughter and gave her a kiss on the top of her head before rustling her hair and walking away. "I appreciate you taking care of me, but you know I can do it myself, right?"

Then he disappeared into the living room.

Chloe grabbed her plate and took it over to the sink.

"It's practice night. Did you want to go to Tony's?"

I looked around the cozy kitchen, the windows fogged up from the pasta steam, the cold black night on the outside. The image of the demon flashed into my brain. Maybe he wasn't the only one looking for me. Maybe I had better be careful. "Or we could just stay here. It's not like I'm a stalker or anything."

Chloe pointed her fork at me and laughed. "Look at you. Maybe you are figuring this out."

15

The minutes dragged into hours, dragged into eternity, until the final school bell rang. The anticipation of seeing Griffin outside of school and the potential of going home—my real home—pumped through my blood. My entire body had twitched all day long, with maximum restlessness occurring in English class when my foot tapped for the entire sixty-minute period as I tried to avoid looking at him. Later, in chemistry, I'd started imagining how our evening would go and I kept dropping beakers, overfilling ingredients, and generally becoming a danger to myself and the entire student body. But what if this was it? What if after tonight I could actually go home?

I sat on the front steps after dinner, waiting for him to show. Red bands of sunset peeked between the houses across the street, and dead leaves twirled and danced across the front lawn. I pulled my sweater closer to my chest.

"What are you looking at?" I asked the lone crow sitting on the fence post beside the driveway.

"Wouldn't you be shocked if he answered?" Chloe chuckled as she tugged the front door closed behind her and hurried down the steps to the front walk.

"Maybe. But at least then I'd know what was so interesting."

"Maybe he thinks you're a bug or something."

"Do I look bad?" I pulled my hair over my shoulder, tugged my fingers through the curls, then adjusted my top.

"You look fine. It's going to be great. And don't be so nervous. If you get back early, I'm going to a movie with Stacey, Brad, and Ashley, then probably off to Tony's if you want to join."

"Thanks. We'll see."

"Have fun," she mocked in a sing-song voice and marched off toward the car.

As she pulled open the driver's side door, a white pickup truck pulled up in front of the house.

"Your prince has arrived." She laughed to herself and got into the driver's seat, closing the door behind her.

I stood up and rushed across the lawn toward the truck. Before I could reach for the passenger door, Griffin ran out and opened it for me.

"Thank you. But maybe I should be opening your door, considering I'm the one who asked."

He smiled, a big wide smile that teased heat into my cheeks. "But I should've asked first."

He climbed back into the driver's seat and headed off down the road, taking a right turn toward the edge of town instead of left like I would have expected. The houses fell away into dark expanses of open fields. Stands of nearly naked trees spotted the landscape. A strange quiver started in my hands—a flash of the night I arrived, naked and in pain. It seemed decades ago now. So much had happened in such a short time.

"Where are we going?" I hid my shaking hands underneath my thighs and slid forward on the truck seat, trying to get a better view through the windshield.

"Not far. Just far enough away from Faraway."

I scanned my brain for words to say but let the radio fill the silence instead. A slow rhythmic beat of guitar and a southern voice, clear and smooth, calmed my anxious soul. There were so many things I wanted to say, so much to discover, but the heaviness of what this could mean clouded over everything. Just a few songs in, Griffin turned the truck off the main road and down a well-worn dirt path shrouded by trees on either side. A cautious flicker started in my stomach, the darkness seeping in and reminding me of the demon who'd attacked me in the music room. A demon who, until the end, looked like anyone else. Just a normal person. I glanced over at Griffin, at the serene look upon his face. This couldn't be a trap, could it?

The road narrowed as we plunged deeper into the unknown, farther and farther away from town and anyone who would be able to hear me scream. Griffin turned down the radio, the eerie silence adding to my impending panic. I glanced around at the floor, beside the seat, even in the truck bed behind us, for anything that might be handy if I'd made a colossal mistake. I eased myself closer to the door, ensuring that the lock was off if I needed to jump.

"Almost there. I hope you're not afraid of a little wilderness?"

"No." I forced my voice still, fighting against the waver building in my throat. "It just seems really far from other people. What if something happens and we need help?"

His forehead crinkled as he squinted in the distance. "I've been out here thousands of times. I'm sure we'll be fine. Besides, I really wanted to be alone with you."

"Ah, okay. But don't you need to be around people? It seems like you're with your team and your friends all the time. I would think you'd want to be somewhere more public."

"Oh. Is that what this is about? I didn't think you were like that."

"Like what?"

"I didn't think you cared about all that. I thought you actually wanted to be with me, not the football player."

I shook my head. "No. I don't care about that. I've never even seen a football game before. I am just making sure you are good."

"Well, considering everyone saw you ask me out, I'm sure they already know where I am tonight. Besides, I didn't want everyone around watching."

"Okay."

"You know what? Maybe this was a bad idea. Maybe I should just take you home." Griffin hit the brake and we stopped in the middle of the road, the dark woods closing in around us.

My mind processed as quickly as it could. Maybe he should take me home? If he'd tricked me, I'd never get home, but if not . . .

"Don't. Please just forget I said anything." A risk, but one I was willing to take.

I held my breath the rest of the drive, devising the best escape plan I could in case I needed it. Eventually the truck veered around a sharp corner and Griffin cut the engine.

Ahead of us spread a sparkling blue lake, calm and crystal under the stars.

"We're here." He jumped from the driver's seat, and before I could get to the door handle, he had opened it for me. "I thought we could have a small bonfire out here. Is that okay?"

Relief settled over me as I jumped down to the gravel below. Griffin reached into the back seat and pulled out a shopping bag. We walked toward a small firepit surrounded by benches made from old tree stumps facing the water. I stopped for a second, took the shopping bag from his hand, and rested it on the ground. I grabbed the zipper of his coat and started pulling it down.

He caught my hand and held it firmly in the middle of his chest. "Wait. What are you doing?"

"Just in case you were worried, I don't care about this jacket. I really just wanted to spend tonight with the apple boy from the farmer's market."

He let go of my hand and I finished opening the zipper. He shrugged the jacket off and placed it back in the truck. The shadow that had fallen over his face lifted, and the light returned to his smile as he picked up the bag, took my hand, and led me over to the firepit.

I sat down on one of the benches and watched as he grabbed logs from a nearby stand and placed them in the metal pit in a kind of pyramid shape. Then he added bunched-up newspaper that he'd brought in the shopping bag and snapped a match. The sour sulfur smell filled the air as he lit the newspaper, and a small glowing fire bounced and danced from the logs.

The heavy smell of burning wood triggered the memory of Seth's arms around me, and I cringed until Griffin sat down beside me and replaced the smell with his own.

"It really is nice here."

Griffin ran the palms of his hands over the thighs of his jeans and gazed out toward the lake. "My dad used to take me fishing here when I was a kid. I guess I've always kind of liked it."

"That's awesome. You two must be pretty close."

"We used to be. But things have been different lately. I don't think we see things the same way anymore."

"Well, that's sad. Is it anything you can fix?"

"I don't know. Sometimes once someone's done something, it can't be undone, you know? It will take me a while before I get over it, I think."

"You don't have to tell me about it, but you can if you want. I've seen a lot of things, and I'm pretty good at listening."

His head hung to his chest and he laced his fingers in front of him. "He cheated. He had a great life with me and my mom, and he cheated on her and broke everything apart."

"I'm sorry."

"Thanks. I spent the last while trying to get over it, but I guess I still haven't. I just don't understand how someone can throw everything away like that."

"Maybe there was a reason. Maybe you don't know the full story. Love seems to make you do crazy things sometimes."

"Yeah, but it didn't have to go like that. He could've left first. He could've moved on and then started seeing someone else. But instead he made the decision to hurt us. Whether he planned on it or not."

"Have you ever told him this?"

"I've tried. But he says he doesn't fully understand either. What kind of answer is that?"

"I don't know."

Griffin put his hands over his face and rubbed them down his cheeks. "I'm sorry about all this. I don't like to talk about it. It's not exactly the best conversation starter."

"It's okay. I think I understand more than you know."

And more than I would ever be able to tell him. Maybe the reason he'd gotten in my brain was because I saw myself. Someone who might understand me, not just condemn.

"I wanted to explain, because it's why I turned you down at first. I've avoided anything to do with relationships since it happened. Just school and football and home."

"Then how come you changed your mind? Why did you say yes?"

"I don't know. There has just been something about you. Something honest that I can't quite explain. But it makes me want to be better. It makes me want to believe that maybe I could find someone who makes me happy."

"I don't know you that well, but so far, you definitely make me happy."

"And you make me happy too." Griffin turned and took my hand, my small fingers disappearing into his wide palms. "But I took you out here for some fun, so let's stop with all the heavy stuff."

He leaned down and pulled a bag of marshmallows, some chocolate bars, and graham crackers from the shopping bag.

"What is all that?"

He raised his left eyebrow in a puzzled look. "It's s'mores. You do know what a s'more is, don't you?"

I shook my head, suddenly embarrassed. "I think I know what they are, but I've never had one."

His head jerked back. "Seriously? You really are city girl, aren't you?"

"Yeah. I guess I don't get out much."

"Well this will be the best thing you have ever had. Trust me, once you've had this, you will be so addicted you are going to beg me to bring you out here all the time."

"Is that a promise?"

His face split into a wide smile. "Yeah, I think it is."

16

"*I* think I'm gonna be sick." I leaned back and rubbed my stomach. The empty bag of marshmallows sat on the bench beside me. "But it might have been worth it."

Griffin peeled the last marshmallow off the roasting stick. The caramelly brown color was absolutely perfect, just as he had been trying to teach me over the past several hours. He popped it in his mouth and licked the sticky residue from his thumb, my eyes unable to avoid staring at his dark red lips. "I told you."

"I guess you're right." I leaned over and nudged him with my shoulder. He laughed, the light joyful sound echoing off the trees. I sat upright again and crossed my arms over my chest, the night air slowly losing its warmth.

"Are you cold?" Without waiting for an answer, he bolted to the truck and ran back with a red and black plaid blanket. He wrapped it around my shoulders. "Better?"

I nodded and grabbed the edges of the blanket, tucking it around me. Ahead of us, the moon reflected a beam of light across the lake. The tiny ripples of minor waves glistened and sparkled, a mirror to the stars that sparkled above it in the sky.

Griffin tossed the roasting stick and the empty marshmallow bag in the fire. He folded his hands behind his head and stared straight up, the mystery of the night drawing him in as well. Or maybe he'd finally run out of things to say. If he felt anything like me, his throat probably burned from talking so much, but if I could redo tonight, I'd take that sting one hundred times over. The evening breeze picked up and started to whistle through the trees. He sat up straighter and pulled his hands into his sleeves, staring down at the small glow of fire smoldering in the metal pit.

I pulled my left arm out and wrapped the long edge of the blanket around his shoulders. He glanced over at me and smiled, sliding closer on the bench so we could both be covered in the fleece.

"Thank you for asking me out and listening to all of my crazy stories," he said, the low rumble of his voice vibrating through my arm as we sat dangerously close together.

"No, they're great."

I pulled my fist, still clutching the blanket, up toward my face to move some stray strands of hair that tickled across my nose.

"Here." He slipped his index finger across my forehead, down over my temple, and around my ear, catching the stray curls and putting them in their place. His touch sparked along my skin, every nerve triggering a happy jolt through my body. He pressed his palm against my cheek, his warm skin like fire against my wind-cold face. He leaned closer and rested his forehead against mine, his lips close—so close that his short, labored breath caressed my mouth. I closed my eyes.

Caw. Caw.

The tree above us rustled loudly and I flipped open my eyes as a crow took off and screamed at the sky. Griffin pulled away, watching the bird fly and chuckling to himself. His hand fell away from my face and into his lap. The farther he moved away from me, the more I deflated.

"I guess someone got tired of watching," I said.

He looked back at me again and grabbed my hand beneath the blanket. "I really want to kiss you."

I squeezed his hand back and shrugged. "Then do it."

Griffin leaned back in, and I breathed in the clean scent of him mixed with the rich smell of wood and chocolate. This was it. Finally.

Caw.

A crow dove right at us, barely missing Griffin's head. He jerked away from me as a second crow swooped down close enough to blow my hair around.

"What the hell?" Griffin yelled as another crow streaked by him again.

I looked up. About twelve crows circled above us, each taking turns to swipe. Griffin covered his head with his arms and one of the birds landed on his elbow, cawing loudly at him. He shook his arm and the bird flew off, rejoining its group.

Griffin grabbed my hand. "Let's get out of here."

He whisked me off the bench, my feet barely

touching the ground before we started to run toward
the truck. The blanket flapped behind me as the birds
continued to swoop at our heads. He raced to the
passenger side and yanked open the door for me, then
ran around to the other side and scrambled in, slamming the door behind him.

He sighed, relief washing over his face, until he
noticed a rip in his sweater where the crow had landed
and clearly torn the fabric. He frowned then shrugged,
likely glad the crow hadn't taken a patch of skin as well.

I pulled the blanket off my back and sank into the
truck seat. "What is going on?"

Griffin stared past me through the passenger
window at the crows still circling. "I don't know. I've
never seen birds act like that before. Maybe there is a
nest or something around here. But it's fall. It shouldn't
be an issue."

I slid across the bench seat and put my hand on his
chest. His heart pumped hard against his ribs, but I
wasn't sure if it was from the crows or the lack of space
between us. Moonlight washed over his face, reflecting
in the calm waters of his eyes, just like the gentle waves
on the lake—but only for me to enjoy. My own private
ocean. He placed his hand over mine and the sparks I'd
felt the day we met returned, crackling under my skin
and heating my cheeks.

Thump.

I jumped as a large crow landed on the truck hood.
Its claws clicked against the metal as it waddled to the
center of the windshield, staring in at us with its red
eyes glowing against the dark shadows of the night.

Griffin squeezed my hand and chuckled as he stared

the bird down then looked back at me. "They can't stop us in here."

He tucked his arm behind me and rested his hand at the nape of my neck. He pulled me closer, his muscles flexing against my sides as he held me tight. Griffin's lips met mine and started to move, the sugary marshmallow tasting sweet on my tongue. And I kissed him back, completely unsure of what to do but savoring in the newness of every sensation. The tingle in my stomach, the sharp, unexpected pain when he accidentally clipped my lip with his teeth, the calm rhythmic sound of our mouths coming together and pulling apart, over and over again.

I wrapped my arms tighter around him, drawing circles into his shoulder blades, kissing him deeper, slipping under the ocean of him. The moon and the stars and the fire fell away into this one perfect moment, and I couldn't even consider going back to Heaven, because in his arms I was already there.

17

"*E*arth to Arianna. Come in, Arianna."

Chloe waved her hand in front of my face as she pulled her car into a parking spot in front of the school.

"Uh, what?" I blinked my eyes, my fingers resting on my lips, still able to feel Griffin there even after an entire night had passed. "Sorry, I'm a little tired. Someone kept me up all night." I glared at Chloe and she laughed, smacking her hand against the steering wheel.

"What did you expect? You burst into my room telling me you made out with Griffin and didn't expect me to ask for all the details?"

"Yeah, but you could have let me go to bed instead of making me repeat them for a third time."

"What can I say, I love the drama." She shrugged and opened the driver's side door, letting the sunny fall morning, and a few stray leaves, into the car.

I sat still for a moment, staring through the windshield, watching the clouds pass. Even if it weren't for the total rehashing with Chloe, I still wouldn't have slept. Once the euphoria of the kiss faded—except it hadn't completely faded yet—my mind wandered back to the reason I'd gone out with Griffin in the first place. I'd tried to fall in love. Tried to book myself a first class ticket back to Heaven. But even though I felt the butterflies and the lightheadedness that every poet and songwriter has gushed about since the beginning of language, I was still here. Raguel had not come for me and time ticked on, closer to the deadline.

The car door opened and I shuddered, being dragged too soon out of my own thoughts.

"Morning." Griffin stood there with a smile bigger than any I'd ever seen since we'd met. "Are you coming in or going to skip this morning?"

I shook my head and climbed out, letting the sun warm my skin, hoping it would melt away the worry burrowing a hole in the back of my brain.

"I needed to find you. I completely forgot to ask you something last night."

"Or maybe you were kinda busy." Chloe snorted.

Griffin's eyes shot daggers at her before he lightened up and chuckled a little himself. "Maybe. But I needed to know if you wanted to go to the homecoming dance with me tomorrow. I know it's short notice, but unless you're going with someone else, I'd love to take you."

I glanced at Chloe, then Griffin, then Chloe again, still unsure of the request, still unsure if I would even be here. "Yeah. I'd like that."

Griffin nodded and grabbed my hand, locking his fingers between mine. We walked toward the doors of the school, Chloe squealing behind us. As we entered the hallway, the familiar stares of everyone fell on my shoulders, but this time they weren't because I was the new girl. By making this move, Griffin had made it clear to everyone that I belonged with him now. We were together.

We reached his locker where the rest of his teammates hovered around like a swarm of purple and yellow bees.

"Good morning, Arianna," Alex said, the level of amusement with the situation evident across his face.

"Good morning, Alex."

"I hope you'll be at the game cheering on our boy. He's been needing a little something this season. Maybe you might just be it."

Griffin opened his locker and grabbed his books, while casting me a private eye roll in response to Alex's smug look.

I laughed, watching the pained look of torture spread across Griffin's face. "Yeah, I'll be there. Wouldn't miss it."

I pushed up on my tiptoes and kissed Griffin on the cheek. His face immediately corrupted into a never-before-seen shade of red. The rest of the guys laughed, but I could see the pride in his expression.

"I'll see you after class," he said as I walked away. The jeers started and I could hear Griffin trying to change the subject.

The glow around me must have been contagious as people smiled and waved, or maybe it was just the first morning I had noticed.

"Are you kidding me?" Seth stood directly in my way, hands on his hips and a scowl across his face. "Did I seriously just have to watch that disgusting scene? Why are you still wasting your time with that ridiculous human?"

"Why are you still wasting your time trying to keep me away from him?"

"I don't care if you're with him, or not, or whatever. This drivel gossip doesn't interest me. I just thought you had bigger priorities." He rolled his eyes toward the ceiling. "A higher calling."

"I do, but it doesn't seem to be working. I still don't know what Raguel wants from me, and I am starting to doubt that he ever planned on taking me back. Maybe its all a big lie."

"But as an angel here on Earth, you're a huge liability. Don't you get that? If I hadn't saved your ass the other day, you would have been dinner for a demon. Do you really think that's what Heaven would want for you? Please tell me you are smart enough to see that."

I stared at the floor, counting the beige specks on the tiles, trying to avoid admitting that Seth had a point. If I didn't leave, they might still come for me—or worse, come for someone else. I wouldn't be able to deal with them hurting any of my new friends. Especially just to get to me.

"Then what do you suggest I do, Seth?"

"Meet me at the game tonight and I can introduce you to someone who can help. Deal?"

I glanced over my shoulder, staring at the lion stitched across Griffin's back. My heart shrank. "Okay. I'm going anyway, so I might as well see what I can do."

Seth's face lit up and he finally stepped out of my way. "You're making the right choice."

"Then why doesn't it feel like it?"

"Because sometimes life is hard. Free will might not really be the gift it's cracked up to be."

"No kidding."

Seth pumped his fist and gave a plastic smile. "Until later. Go Lions."

18

The stadium hummed with enough energy to light the world for a week. Fourth quarter, seven minutes left, 28–28. I still didn't understand half the calls, but I'd picked up the general idea. Get the ball past the line without getting tackled to the ground. A simple premise, but a much harder task in reality. On the sidelines at least three of the Lions nursed injuries from what looked like painful attacks. Painful enough that the collective audience felt it.

On the other side of the field, the blue sea of Bartlett Bears fans cheered and screamed as loud, if not more, than our purple Faraway Lions fans. Unfortunately, in this game the purple stood for bruising.

Chloe watched intently as the quarterback threw the ball and another player near the side of the field caught it before getting trampled by one of the Bartlett Bears.

"Oh, come on! Where's the call?" she shouted, flipping a hand in the air then turning toward me and smiling like she hadn't just screamed at the official. She was right. People here really loved their football.

I loosened the yellow and purple scarf around my neck and clapped my hands along with the bubbly cheer squad, desperately trying to rally support for our battered team.

"At least it's a pretty good game." Seth had somehow managed to slip beside me as if by way of magic. But knowing him, it was likely just by being a bit slippery.

"I thought we were meeting after the game."

"Yeah. But I'm allowed to have a little fun once in a while too, you know." He stuck his lip out in a pouty frown, his eyes too amused to sell it.

Chloe glanced over and saw him standing beside me. She rolled her eyes. From the look of disgust on her face I wouldn't have been surprised to see her march right out of the stadium—except that would mean she'd miss the end of the game. Clearly, I'd found her one true weakness.

Seth leaned over and shouted in my ear. "Unless you want to get out of here early. I am so okay with that."

"Thanks, but I want to stay."

"What is it with you and these humans anyway? Didn't you get tossed for messing with them? Now here you are just begging for any excuse to hang out with them."

"And what exactly did you do to end up here, Seth? You've never really told me your story. Why am I always the one who has to share information?"

His face blanched in spite of the piercing fall wind. "That's fair. Once we get out of here, I'll tell you."

"Why not now? Why wait?"

"Because I can barely hear you right now. Unless you'd rather take this somewhere else?"

I glanced at Chloe, then the clock. Less than a minute and everyone would be piling out of here like rats escaping a burning building. I likely wouldn't miss much at this point.

"Fine."

I tapped Chloe on the shoulder to tell her that I would find her later, but at that second Griffin caught the ball and started to run. I stood there, mouth open, watching him barrel down the field faster than I'd ever seen anyone run. One of the Bears tried to get in his way, but our Lion guards picked him off and gave Griffin a clear path. Thirty yards. Twenty yards. Ten yards. I squeezed my fists and stood on my toes, every muscle in my body clenching tight. Five yards. Touchdown! Chloe screamed and jumped up and down. She turned and grabbed my arms, and I started jumping with her. The entire Lions' bleachers erupted in cheers and screams.

The team lined up again and kicked the ball through the metal goalpost. The cheering grew louder—a feat I'd thought would not be possible.

"We won!" Chloe screamed over and over. "We won!"

Seth sat uninterested in the entire event, picking at his fingernails and somehow ignoring the chaos around him. I glanced down at the field. Griffin pulled his helmet off and his team surrounded him. He'd done it.

As the team thinned, he turned to the stands and waved. To me? To everyone? The strange feeling burning in my chest wanted it to be me. Wanted him to want to celebrate with me. Maybe Seth was right, and I'd gone too far down the human road.

"That was awesome," Chloe said as she patted me on the back and we filed out of the row, moving ever so slowly with the mass of people trying to exit. "Remind me not to mock your guy for at least a week. He deserves a bit of credit."

"Can we go now?" Seth interrupted as he was nearly bulldozed down the stairs by a middle-aged man and his three children. Seth scowled at them and proceeded on.

"Can we wait a little bit? I want to talk to Griffin first. What if I don't get another chance?"

The heaviness of the words burned my tongue as they came out of my mouth. Why did the thought of going home suddenly make me sad?

Seth scoffed. "I'm sure he's going to be a while. They'll be celebrating in the locker room, and by the time he's done, it'll be halfway to midnight."

"But I'll be able to come back, right? I'll be able to see everyone before—" I glanced back, but Chloe wasn't paying attention, "—to say goodbye?"

"Of course. But I don't want you to lose another chance."

I turned back to Chloe. "Can I meet you in the parking lot in a few minutes?"

"What's up?"

"Seth wants me to meet someone, and then I want to say congratulations to Griffin."

"Sure. It'll be hell getting out of here anyway. At least for a little while. But if you get a ride with someone else, make sure they text me, okay?"

I stopped and hugged her, wrapping my arms as

tightly around as I could. She'd been kind when she didn't need to be. She'd been my friend, even though I probably didn't deserve it. I'd miss her so much.

"What's wrong?" she asked.

"Nothing." I wiped the back of my arm across my face, the wind chilling the corners of my eyes where tears had started to form. "I'm just not good with crowds."

I followed Seth out into the field behind the stadium as the mob continued toward the parking lot.

"So where is this guy?"

"He was supposed to be here. Let me go check." Seth ran off toward the school.

I stood alone in the dark. At least it was an open field and I could see anyone coming if I needed to. I wrapped my arms tightly around myself to keep the chill away. The reality that this might be my last night on Earth made me oddly melancholy. I wanted to go home. I missed my wings. I missed the other angels. The power. The only life I'd ever known. I even sort of missed Raguel. But losing my friends here burned through my veins like acid burning away my old life and replacing it with the new.

Seth jogged back and shone his phone at me, the text screen lit like a firefly in the dark. "He said to meet him at the front of the school. Let's go."

The stadium had cleared quickly, and I shivered at the emptiness it left behind.

"Hurry up. We don't want to keep him waiting."

I rushed behind Seth, trying my best to keep pace, but my head wasn't letting my feet move as fast as they should.

"It'll be faster if we cut through over here," Seth said and darted under the bleachers, weaving in and out of metal posts.

I struggled to keep up then—*bang*—smacked into Seth as he stopped.

"Whoa." He turned around and tried to shuffle me out of the way. "Let's go a different way."

A light giggle echoed under the bleachers. I glanced over his shoulder. Long waves of silky raven hair fell from the back of the giggle girl's head. Her arms reached above her, tangled around the neck of a taller brown-haired boy in a purple and yellow Lions jacket. She laughed again, tossing her hair back then leaning in for a kiss.

I clasped my hand over my mouth and moved sideways with Seth, hoping we hadn't disturbed them. At least someone was going to have a good evening. I crept back, trying to get out as quickly as possible, but as I turned my head to go, something caught in my periphery and stung inside my brain. The number on the sleeve. Two stitched numbers that sank my entire world. Number 62. Griffin wore number 62.

19

*S*he looked like the kind of girl Griffin should be kissing. Tall, beautiful, with dark silky hair to the middle of her back and the cutest skirt and sweater combo in the school's definitive purple and yellow. And they looked amazing, with her arms wrapped tightly around his neck, standing on her tippy toes to reach his full lips, while slowly twisting the knife that plunged into my chest the second I saw those two numbers. 62. The number of pieces my heart crumbled into.

"Wait. Isn't he your boyfriend?" Seth stood beside me, his jaw wide open. The same shock as mine but running much less deep. He pointed his finger toward them. "Hey, Griff, aren't you the stud today."

Griffin pulled the girl off him and shook his head. "Arianna?"

I didn't respond. Instead I turned away, not willing to show him the tears threatening to fall. He didn't get to take pleasure in my pain.

He rushed up behind me and put his hand on my shoulder.

"What?" I spat at him without turning around.

"I don't know what happened. I swear. She kissed me. Out of nowhere. You know I wouldn't do something like this. Not to you, not to anyone."

"Do I? Maybe it was all just some line? Did you tell her the same lies to get her attention?"

"No. There's nothing with me and that girl. I don't even know her name."

"Wow, that's classy," Seth said from the sidelines.

"Why don't you just get lost? This has nothing to do with you."

"It does when you think you can just hurt people like that."

Griffin rushed over to Seth and grabbed him by the collar. "I'm telling you, I didn't kiss that girl. She kissed me. It's all kind of fuzzy."

"Fuzzy? Isn't that convenient."

"Why, I oughta—"

"Enough!" I whirled around and Griffin let go of Seth. "I don't know what to believe right now. Just leave me alone."

I ran off toward the parking lot. I needed to find Chloe. I needed to get out of there. A burning sensation started in the back of my throat as the chicken and pota-toes we had for dinner threatened to come back for a second taste. The lot was a mass of cars, so I stood back and scanned the crowd, trying to find her. I looked for her bright purple scarf, but everyone wore some shade of purple, which didn't help. I placed my hand on my forehead, heat bubbling in my blood. How could he do that? Had everything he'd said to me been a lie? Did he even care about me at all? No wonder our kiss didn't send me back—he'd never felt it anyway.

Seth ran up beside me and rested his arm over my shoulders. "Are you okay?"

I wanted to shrug him off—I didn't want anyone to touch me—but I couldn't seem to get my brain to stop thinking enough to move my body.

"I need to go home."

"Let me help you. I told you before, humans aren't worth it. They are such a disaster."

"But I thought . . . I thought he was different."

"None of them are. But I can help. I know someone who can take away all this pain, all this misery. Someone who wouldn't make you suffer like this."

"I don't know. I don't know anything right now. I can't even think."

"Which is why you need to make this decision. Choose to come with me and I'll show you. Make the choice to choose yourself over them. You don't have to go back to Heaven. There are better options for people like you. Ones that don't involve stupid tests."

"Wait." My head throbbed as his words clicked together in my brain. Too many boys with their broken promises for one night. "I thought you said you would help me get back."

"I said I knew someone who could help you, but you don't need to go back, Arianna."

"Enough." I finally focused my energy enough to push Seth away. "I have just more than one day left to figure out what Raguel meant or I will be stuck on this stupid planet forever. I'm an angel, Seth. Wings, halo, fallen straight from the sky. You know that. I can't just decide to do something else. I need to find a way to get back to Heaven where I belong."

"You're a what?"

I looked over to see Chloe standing beside us, her car keys dangling from her index finger.

"There you are. I've been looking all over for you." I walked toward her, but she stepped back, her hands held out in front of her, the color draining from her face as she shook her head at me.

"Don't come anywhere near me. Is it true? You're not human, you're an angel?"

I nodded and stared down at the ground, kicking the tufts of grass with my sneaker. "I wanted to tell you, but I . . . I couldn't."

"You couldn't tell me, but you could tell him." She jerked her head at Seth, her stare sharp enough to cut glass. "Real nice."

Seth shrugged and glanced at me, smart enough to push down his amusement, but just barely.

"I didn't tell him. He already knew."

The rage burning in her eyes faded into something darker. Something sad.

"Chloe. I'm so sorry." I reached out to touch her, to connect with her somehow and make things okay like she always did for me, but she stomped past and into the parking lot.

"If you still need a ride, I'm going home," she hissed. The harsh edge to her voice wavered.

I followed quickly behind, but Seth grabbed my arm.

"Let her go. You need to worry about yourself."

I tugged myself away. "Not right now. I need to deal with this."

I raced toward the car and jumped into the passenger seat as Chloe stomped on the gas, the door barely closing before she lurched forward into traffic.

"I'm so sorry I didn't tell you. I just didn't know what to say. Or if you would have even believed me."

"You never planned on staying, did you? You were just here for a few days to take what you wanted and then you'd be gone."

"I never wanted to hurt you, Chloe."

"Well, how did you think I was going to feel when I opened your door one morning and you were just gone? Were you even going to say goodbye, or were you just going to disappear?"

"I hadn't really thought that far ahead."

"Well, how long did you have then?"

"Until tomorrow." I hung my head and stared at my fingers twisted in my lap. The disappointment rolled off Chloe's skin and filled the air between us.

"So, just a week. And everything you told me, everything you said, I can assume is all lies?"

"No, I meant what I said. I interfered with humans when I wasn't supposed to. It's the number one rule of angels, but I did it anyway. I was sent here to experience what it's like to be human. To learn how to be human."

She stared out the windshield, her knuckles white as she gripped the steering wheel, her braking too heavy and her turns too sharp to be okay. But I much preferred her yelling at me. At least then I knew what she was thinking.

We pulled into the driveway. She jammed the car

into park, turned off the engine, and jumped out, slamming the driver's side door behind her. I slowly crept out of the car, unsure of what to say next, knowing that nothing would make her feel better. Nothing would make up for my lies.

"I think I'm going to take a walk. Will you come with me?" I stuffed my hands in my pockets, hoping she would take the invitation. Let me have a chance to explain.

She rushed up the front steps, the screen door in her hand, then she paused and hung her head. "Why? Clearly you have bigger issues to deal with that don't involve me. It's probably better if you said goodbye now since you'll be leaving soon anyway. You're just like everyone else. I should've known you'd just leave."

"That's not—"

But there was no point in arguing. Chloe slipped inside the door and disappeared.

20

I dug my toes into the gravel and pushed myself forward on the swing. The weathered chains creaked loudly and shrilly in the dark. Back and forth. Back and forth. Swinging into the night breeze, as I replayed the events of the night over and over again.

That girl's arms wrapped around Griffin's neck, his lips pushed against hers.

Kiss.

The cold, disappointed shadow that fell across Chloe's face as she clicked the front door shut, leaving me in the driveway.

Click.

Each image crashed over me. Dangerous waves on a distant shore. My body reacting to each blow, every muscle tightening, every breath a labor.

Cringe.

Over and over, just like the swing, in a constant loop of never getting anywhere.

Kiss. Click. Cringe.

Tears escaped my eyes, plastering against my cheeks as I sailed through the air. A murder of crows flew in and perched on the top of the slide, staring with their red beady eyes as I pumped my feet and rose higher and higher into their sky.

Kiss. Click. Cringe.

One last big push and I jumped from the swing at its highest peak, my eyes closed, urging my wings to open and carry me away. But instead I fell to the ground and a jolt of pain pierced through my ankles, knocking me to my knees.

Half the crows scattered, cawing at the moon about the crazy angel who couldn't fly. One of the larger crows sailed down to the ground and hopped toward me, closer, his tiny head cocked to the left as if I were the strange one.

I slammed my hand against the ground. "Get out of here. Go away."

It didn't listen. Just hopped slower, pausing in its movements but not changing course. I grabbed a rock from the ground and chucked it in the bird's direction, just to the right, but close enough. It startled, its stare searing into my head. Blaming me. Knowing I'd been the one to throw it. As if to mock me, it extended its onyx feathers and squawked, then burst into the sky with a flap of fury.

I pushed myself up to my feet and stared after it. But it was gone.

Kiss. Click. Cringe.

The loop began again. And the tears began to flow.

"I'm done," I yelled into the sky, my arms open at my sides. "Did you hear that, Raguel? I've done everything you've asked. I've come here, I've been human, I fell in love. I get it now. No need to keep punishing me.

"These people. They hurt each other. They hurt themselves. I don't know what more you want from me. You need to take me back. I want to go back."

I wiped my eyes with the back of my sleeve, but it made no difference. Tears poured down my face as I struggled to breathe between gasps. If love was simply a trick—a tool that people used against each other—then I was over it.

"I won't do it again, I promise. I'll let them destroy each other. Let them live their lives without interfering. I don't care what they do anymore. Just please, Raguel, please take me back."

The sound of rustling leaves. The wind whipping through empty fields. Whispers of the earth, but no Raguel.

"Do you even hear me?" I screamed, the words ripping themselves up my throat, echoing in the open air.

"I doubt they'll listen when you talk like that," a voice said behind me.

I whirled around as Margaret stepped into the playground. James stood guard on the sidewalk, his hands thrust deep into his pockets.

"How did you know to find me here?"

"I saw you." Her thin lips curled into a mischievous smile. "And I doubt you really want to be remembered as the girl who tried to yell at Heaven."

"I don't know what to do." I buried my face in my hands and walked toward her.

"There, there, dear." She wrapped her arms around

me, her limbs shaking as she pulled my wet face into her shoulder. "Few of us ever know what we're doing. That's part of the magic."

"I thought I had it figured out. I looked for love just like Raguel said, and I thought I had found it. But now everything is ruined. Griffin kissed someone else, and Chloe . . . Chloe hates me."

"Well then, you're lucky, aren't you?"

"What?" I pulled my face from her sweater; the faint wisp of lavender filled the space between us.

"It sounds as though you've made some good connections here. Been impacted."

"Didn't you just hear me? Nothing is working out. I'm running out of time and everything is falling apart."

"But, maybe *you* don't quite understand. People can only hurt us if we care for them. If we love them. When you don't care, it doesn't hurt. If the reason you are truly upset is because you can't return to Heaven, then you have learned nothing. But if these tears are for the friends you've made, then maybe you still stand a chance."

"But what if I don't? What if all this was for nothing and I ruined my chances of going home?"

"Then I guess you need to spend more time seeing what's right in front of you. Or, you need to start accepting the fact that you may never be an angel again."

"I don't think I can do it."

"Some days, neither do I, but I do. And you will too. Now, dry those eyes, stop blaming the heavens, and get back out there. People may still surprise you. You might even surprise yourself."

She straightened my hair behind my ear and down

my back, then gave my shoulder a quick squeeze before James appeared at her side and took her hand.

"What do I do now?" I asked as they slowly walked up the street toward their car.

Margaret turned around. "Stop trying to act like a human and let yourself be one."

I watched the car disappear around the corner and took one last look up at the bluish light of the moon filtering through the clouds. Heaven seemed farther away than ever.

21

*A*ll the lights were dark when I opened the front door to the house. I glanced at the clock on the microwave in the kitchen. 12:52. I crept down the hallway to Chloe's room and peeked in at her purple comforter with the large body-shaped lump in the middle, her soft blond hair splayed out in waves on her pillow.

"Chloe?" I said to the moonlit room.

No answer. Either she'd fallen asleep or still didn't want to speak to me. I tried again, but she didn't flinch.

I quietly closed the door and headed back down the hall. In my periphery, I noticed the lamp still on in the living room. I snuck in and clicked it off, leaving Stephen sleeping in his favorite chair.

"Good night," I whispered to the air.

"You're home?"

I froze, not expecting a response. "Yeah. Just going to bed."

"The Carlisle boy was here for you, and then he called about ten times."

"Thanks."

Bile rose in the back of my throat. The thought of Griffin. Here. All of the horrible thoughts came flooding back. The pretty girl with her pretty lips.

"Just one thing. I don't know what happened tonight, and I doubt I really want to know, but if you do anything to make my Chloe cry like that again, I think you will need to find a new place to stay. Understood?"

The room spun and closed in around me, my breathing getting difficult as I choked back my own tears. I'd hurt her. I knew I had. But hearing it made it real. "Understood. I didn't mean for—"

"I don't want to know. I just want to know that you are looking out for my daughter."

"I am, sir. She's the best friend I've ever had."

"Then remember how fortunate you are to have people like her in your life. Now go get some sleep."

I SPRANG up in bed as the door creaked open. Through my sleepy haze the image of Chloe standing in the doorway became clear, her long hair draped over her shoulders like a ghost standing guard over my bed.

"Are you awake?" she asked.

I rubbed my face, still unsure if I was talking to a spirit or if it was really her. "Yeah."

She slipped in quietly, the near silent footfalls whispering until she reached the side of the bed and sat down.

I moved upright and pulled my knees toward my chest. "Are you still mad at me?"

"A little. I don't like that you lied to me, but I understand why you had to."

The weight that had been pushing against my rib cage since the second she had stormed away from me lifted, if only a fraction.

"I didn't mean to hurt you."

"I know." She tilted her head toward the window, and the blue moonlight fell across her face. Glassy, glistening streaks of tears tainted her cheeks, hidden before in the dark, now highlighted for me to see. "But can I ask you a question?"

I linked my arm in hers, hoping she wouldn't push me away, wanting to be close to her. Help her forgive me. "Sure."

"What's it like?" she whispered, her voice wavering.

"What do you mean?"

"In Heaven. Is it nice up there?" She coughed on her words, her voice finally breaking. "Do you think she's happy? My mom? Do you think my mom is happy up there?"

A fresh stream slid down her left cheek. My heart broke in my chest as her spirit did before my eyes.

I wrapped my arm around her shoulder, and she let me. "It's wonderful. I think she would be very happy. There would be no pain. No more hurt. But I'm sure she misses you every day."

"Have you met her? Do you know for sure?"

"I haven't. There are millions of people there. But if she's anything like you, I can guarantee that she's among them." I clutched tighter on her shoulder, as if to hold her together, as stray tears spilled onto my leg.

"Can you do me a favor?"

"Anything. Whatever you want."

"When you get back, can you find her for me? Find her and tell her that I'm sorry I blamed her. Sorry that I was angry that she died."

"I'm sure she already knows."

She turned her face to me, her destroyed look ripping me apart. "But can you tell her anyway?"

"Of course. I will search until I find her. Even if it takes forever."

"Thank you," she whispered.

She curled up in my lap, and I ran my fingers through her hair. She didn't speak for a long time but fought back the haggard breaths as the tears rolled long into the morning.

he wicked sun streamed in across my face. I rubbed my eyes and propped myself up on my elbows, still expecting to see Chloe at the edge of my bed, but the bunched-up comforter sat there instead. My ribs tightened around my lungs, my breath trapped inside and aching as I remembered oceans of her tears flooding onto my shoulder.

I flopped back down and turned my head to glance at the alarm clock on the dresser. 11:13 on the last day of my punishment. What did that even mean? When the end of the day came, would I simply disappear? Become dust that floated along forever in pieces? What if nothing happened, and I simply remained here in this world with no chance of returning home? There was no way I'd ever reach Raguel's goals now. Griffin had deceived me, and I had deceived Chloe. The only two people I truly trusted. Maybe I could stay if Chloe would let me? Maybe I belonged in this house of broken hearts, three fools destined for sadness.

A little knock rapped on the door.

"Are you awake?" Chloe whispered as she pushed the door wider.

"Uh-huh." I sat up and pulled my knees to my chest, giving her room to sit down. The marks on her face had faded, and her freshly washed hair was the only thing still sopping wet.

She crept in and flopped on the end of the bed, leaning her back against the wall and stretching her legs over the side.

"How are you doing?" I asked as my arms trembled, fearing the answer.

"Better."

"You know I never meant to hurt you, right?"

"I do." She nodded and closed her eyes as a knowing smile fluttered across her lips. "So how are you doing?"

"Fine. I was just worried about you."

"There's nothing you can change now. You can only move forward. But really, I talked to Griffin last night and heard what happened. If I were you, I'd be pretty upset."

I pulled my legs tighter, holding my body into itself, letting the grief of disappointing Chloe fade enough to let my disappointment in Griffin overtake it. "I guess I just wanted it to work so badly I didn't realize that I was so wrong."

"I'm not so sure about that. It's entirely up to you, but I kind of believe him. I don't really want to, because it sounds pretty bad, but he was a huge wreck when he showed up here last night, and from the way he looks at you, to him, I don't think any other girl exists."

"Maybe. But I'm sure it's over now."

"He asked me to give you this." She reached into the pocket of her sweatpants and pulled out a folded sheet of paper. The ragged edges were curly from being ripped from a spiral notebook.

With shaking fingers, I unfolded it.

Ari,

I am so sorry. I swear to you that I am telling you the truth. I never kissed that girl. I barely even remember what happened, just leaving the dressing room then that devastated look on your face. I don't know if you can forgive me, but if you can, I'll be waiting. Call me, text me, whatever, but just let me explain. Also, if you'd still be willing to go to the homecoming dance with me, I would be the luckiest guy in the room.

Always your boy with the apples,
   Griffin

I CAREFULLY FOLDED the letter and placed it on the dresser, then hung my head toward my chest. "I don't know."

"For what it's worth, I think you should at least hear him out, but it's your choice." Chloe slid onto her knees and crawled up beside me, resting her head on my shoulder and her arm around me, a mirror of not even five hours before when I was the one to comfort her.

"Either way, we can still go to the dance and have a

good time. You definitely don't need some guy to feel pretty and enjoy yourself."

"But I wouldn't want to interfere with your date with Brad."

"You wouldn't. Besides, if anything is gonna happen between us, it will. Right now I want to spend as much time with my friend before she leaves."

"You're a truly good person, Chloe Martin."

"Aw." She rubbed my arm, easing the blackness falling over my thoughts.

"Now, are you going to homecoming with me or not?"

"Well, I don't think there's a dress in that suitcase, so unless you want me there in sweatpants, I should probably stay here."

"You can borrow something of mine. I doubt you'd want to hang out all night with my dad."

Chloe bounded up to her feet, off the edge of the bed, and ran down the hallway. I stretched and stood, then looked myself over in the mirror. I looked like I hadn't slept in a thousand years, but who knew after tonight if I would ever need sleep again.

Chloe rushed back into the room with a delicious smirk across her face. "I know I said you could borrow something of mine but . . ." She pulled her hand out from behind her back to reveal a short white gown hanging from a black velvet hanger.

"It's beautiful." I stepped forward and traced my fingers over the thin rhinestone belt and fluffed the layers of white chiffon.

Chloe shook the hanger at me. "My mom saw it in the store once and couldn't resist buying it. She said she wanted to save it for a special occasion, but she never did get a chance to wear it. Try it on."

"I couldn't."

"Of course, you can. I think it will fit you perfectly."

"But it's your mom's."

"And she would have loved to see someone enjoy it."

Chloe undid the zipper on the side and I pulled it over my head. The white satin straps dipped to a stunning sweetheart neckline, pulling gently around my curves. The dreamy skirt hit just above the knee, like someone had hand-sewn this dress, waiting for me to come.

Chloe adjusted the straps down my back, her fingers brushing over my scars.

"Is this where . . . ?"

"Yes. I wish you could see them. They are magnificent."

"I'll bet. But, maybe we should keep your hair down, to avoid any questions."

"Good idea."

She swept my scruffy slept-on hair forward over the front of the dress, and I could picture how elegant I would look with the help of a hairbrush and maybe a little lip gloss. As she pulled her hands away, I spun around, letting the layers swish around me.

"Just what I said. Perfect. If you can't be an angel, you might as well look like one."

I pulled Chloe close and squeezed, her arms slowly squeezing me back. "Thank you. You're probably twice the angel I ever was."

"No problem. That's what friends do."

23

*C*hloe pulled open the back door of Brad's Civic hatchback, freeing me from the back seat.

"Well, thank you, mademoiselle."

She extended her hand through the doorway and I accepted as the night air pulsed in waves crashing over each other, again and again, as a synthetic electronic bass line pumped through the glass doors of the school.

"Are you ready?" Brad rushed around the side of the car, slipping his hand around Chloe's waist. They looked charming together. Brad's attempt at dapper, with a three-piece black suit, worked with his dark wavy hair and crooked grin. And Chloe—Chloe shone like the stars, dazzling in a long blush halter dress that floated around her when Brad twirled her in the parking lot. Her simple silver bracelet caught the light of the street-lamps and added unnecessary sparkle as her smile lit up the night.

"Yes. I can't wait." She slipped her arm in his and they walked toward the front steps of the school.

Part of me considered going back to the house and sitting on the back deck, waiting for whatever may come, but I promised her I would be here, so here I was. Maybe if things didn't go well, I could slip out the back and leave them alone.

"Hurry up, Arianna," Chloe said as she turned and waved her hand at me. The soft curly tendrils that framed her face drifted in the evening breeze. She looked like a movie star who had just stepped down from the screen.

"Just a sec." I closed my eyes and twiddled my fingers, letting out a huge breath. Now or never.

I rushed across the lot to catch up with them, wishing I had passed up Chloe's offer of heels. They were a good inch shorter then hers, but for an angel I had the grace of a baby giraffe.

As I approached, Brad and Chloe stepped out of the way, revealing Griffin in a steel-blue suit sitting on the front steps, his fingers laced together in front of him.

"You came." Griffin stood up and shoved his hands into his pockets, keeping his distance and staring down at his shoes.

I nodded, though I doubt he saw. The blood rushed to my temples as I looked him over. The jacket cut right across his broad shoulders and tapered gently to his waist, accentuating the strong muscular arms I knew were hidden underneath. His stark-white collar and sleek brushed-up hairstyle gave him an unexpected polish, elevating him from classically handsome to elegantly gorgeous. Just like the prince Chloe said he was that first day at school. But I shouldn't care. It didn't matter how he looked. What mattered was how he'd deceived me.

"Well," Chloe glanced at Brad with a warm smile, "we'll see you guys inside. If you need anything, Arianna, just come get me."

Griffin watched them walk away, leaning back on his heels then swinging forward to his toes and back again. "I wasn't sure if you got my note. You didn't call, so I started to think you weren't going to show."

"You aren't keeping your other date waiting?"

"No. I told you there is no one else." He reached forward to take my hand, but I stepped back and dug it into the chiffon near my leg.

"I'm serious. I am so sorry for what happened, but you have to believe me. That wasn't something I would do. After all I told you about my dad and how betrayed I felt, do you honestly think I would do something like that?"

I didn't. In my heart I didn't believe he would do something like that, which was probably why it burned in my lungs like the sting of drowning—unable to escape no matter how hard I swam, the dark murky depths closing in around me.

"How can you explain what I saw then?"

"I can't. All I remember is leaving the locker room and coming around to the back of the school. Then your friend told me to meet you by the bleachers, and the next thing I knew you were standing there staring at me with tears in your eyes."

"My friend?"

"Yeah. That Seth guy that's always hanging around you. The one who told me to meet you."

Seth. What did he have to do with this? For some reason something didn't seem right. Could Griffin really be telling the truth?

"I really want to believe you."

He stepped closer, his endless stare locking on mine. It was the first time he dared to look at me. "Give me another chance. I swear to you nothing like this will ever happen again. I don't know how it happened in the first place, but I will do whatever I can to make it up to you. The moment we first met, there was something about you. I can't shake you no matter how hard I try. I didn't want anyone in my life. It was too difficult—too much for me to handle—but I can't think about not having you around. You're amazing, Ari, and I think I might be falling in love with you."

My knees quivered beneath my skirt and my blood raced through my veins, sparking energy through my limbs, waking up every cell, every nerve. This wasn't just a test. Somewhere along the way I had actually fallen for him too. Now, I didn't know where to go from here.

"Maybe I can give you another chance. Maybe not right away, but I'll try."

He nodded. "I can work with that. I know who I am, and what I stand for, and I will prove that to you."

I pulled my arms tighter to my body, rubbing my palms over my exposed arms as the night breeze intensified. "Can we go inside now?"

"Of course." He stepped aside, letting me lead, and rested the palm of his hand on the small of my back, sending sparks up my spine. I reached behind and grabbed his hand, pulling it beside me and threading my fingers through his. He smiled and lifted our hands to his lips to place a slow, warm kiss on the top of mine.

"Thank you," he whispered. "You won't regret this."

24

We stepped into the gym, or what might have been the epicenter of a glitter bomb. Twinkling white lights and silver stars hung between strands of tulle streamers, transforming the sweaty athletic center into something almost beautiful. The music pounded into the front of my chest and burrowed its way through the other side.

Griffin leaned toward my ear. "I can already tell that I'm with the most beautiful girl here."

"Stop trying so hard. Just be you. That's all I've ever wanted."

"Okay. But it's still true. Did you want to dance or something?"

"Sure, that would be—"

"Griff!" Alex yelled from the corner, waving his hand at us. "Over here."

Griffin ignored him and kept leading me toward the dance floor.

"Griff!" he yelled again.

Griffin's arm sagged as he sighed. "Do you mind if I go talk to the guys for a minute? Then I'm yours for the rest of the night. Promise. They won't let up unless I acknowledge them."

"Sure. Go ahead."

His eyebrows turned up and he grabbed my hand again. "You can come with me."

"Actually, I want to try to find Chloe and let her know I'm here. If I don't, she might come after you."

He laughed. "I wouldn't want that. I have a strange feeling that she could probably knock me out if she had the chance. I'll just be a minute."

I scanned the gym. Even in heels and pushed onto my tiptoes, I still couldn't see over all the heads in the room. I should have been able to pick her out, but there were just too many people.

An arm wrapped around my waist as an odd sinister shadow fell over me.

"Do I get a dance?" a deep raspy voice whispered in my ear.

The arm gripped my hip and swirled me around. My balance wavered as I fell forward, face to face with Seth. I stiffened at the sight of him as my brain tried to reconcile the version of Seth I thought I knew with the one that might have tried to sabotage Griffin.

"Hey. I didn't know you were coming."

"Of course. Wouldn't miss a chance to see everyone acting like idiots."

"Is that why you dressed up?" I eyed his carefully slicked-back hair and pressed-black dress shirt, casually unbuttoned at the collar. It seemed out of place for him yet exactly his style. Blending in, but just a bit different from everyone else.

He leaned over and whispered in my ear. "No. I did that for you."

My pulse quickened and I stepped back, but his arm caught my waist again, his right hand sliding into mine.

"I better not. I'm here with Griffin."

"Just because he's your date doesn't mean he owns you. Besides, I'm sure it wouldn't be hard for someone like him to find another date. Oh wait—isn't that what he was doing last night with that hot girl dangling from his face?" He frowned then tried to turn it into a playful smirk, but the malice still curled at the edges of his lips.

"Watch it, Seth. I don't think this is a good idea." I tried to pull my hand from his, but he clamped on tighter, my knuckles pinching against one another as his other hand dug into my lower back.

"I'm serious. Let me go or I'll scream."

"Now, why would you go and do something foolish like that? Haven't you caused enough drama since you've been posing as a human? Besides, I've sent demons after you, spelled your witless beau into kissing another girl right in front of you—yet you still hopelessly believe that Heaven will save you. You are way out of your league here."

My throat dried—all of the moisture suddenly sucked out of the air. "You did this to me. I thought you said you wanted to help me."

Seth tossed his head back and laughed. More of a cackle, dark and wicked. "Isn't that sweet. I know you've felt off since you met me, and your instincts weren't wrong. If you'd just let yourself accept them. I've been watching you since the second you hit the earth. Planning. Waiting. Angels don't fall every day, you know."

I wriggled in his grip again, but he held firm. I glanced over my shoulder. Griffin stood across the room, still talking to his football friends, oblivious to what was happening.

"I tried to make this easy on you. But you just kept refusing to give in." Seth's stare burrowed into my skull, and for the briefest flash his eyes glowed red. Bright as fresh blood. "I serve a different power. One that can free you from all of these ridiculous divine rules. Your master may have abandoned you, but mine never would. He has bigger plans. Plus, he seems to have a special interest in fallen angels. Maybe because he's one himself."

Breath left my body in a loud gasp that no one could hear over the pounding music. I grabbed Seth's wrist with my free hand and dug my nails in as hard as I could.

"Ow! You witch."

I swung my foot forward and dug the stiletto heel into the fleshy part where his ankle met his leg. His grip relaxed enough for me to pull myself away. I turned and ran toward the door, kicking off my shoes for an extra burst of speed.

I peeled down the hallway. Seth's heavy footfalls echoed behind me, but I refused to look back. It would only slow me down. I hit the main doors and flew over the front steps toward the parking lot, grit and gravel digging into the soles of my feet. But I kept running. To where, I didn't know.

As I neared the far end of the lot, a crow flew at me. I

ducked my head so it wouldn't slam into the back of my skull. It landed on a dumpster and turned to stare, its glowing red eyes stopping me in my tracks. It squawked then jumped off the side, floating down to the concrete. As its clawed feet touched down, its oil-slick wings spread larger and larger, extending up into the sky. A wisp of smoke swirled around its bird body as its feathers fell and disappeared. The smoke thickened so I couldn't see through it, then vanished in a strong gust. Instead of the crow, Seth stood before me, his eyes still burning crimson.

25

"So that means you're—"

"A demon? Of course. But I doubt I could have come right out and told one of Heaven's finest without repercussions."

He stepped forward and I stepped back, a reflexive dance of repulsion and fear.

"Besides, if I had told you, you never would've trusted me. And I needed you to trust me. If you had, then maybe things would have been better. They wouldn't have to go this way."

A flapping of wings filled the air as crows descended on the parking lot in front of me, beside me, behind me. Wafts of purple smoke arose, revealing an army of demons watching Seth's every move. Beside him, the demon that had tried to attack me in the music room appeared, and on his other side the dark-haired beauty that had kissed Griffin.

"You set me up. All these things that happened—the

terrible things—were just a way to get closer to me. You even fought off your own kind. But for what?"

"I told you. A war is coming, and one day it will ravage this earth. It will devour all of humankind as a final match between the angels and the demons, and right now we need all the assistance we can get."

Seth's red eyes burned through me as he stepped closer. I tried to back up again, but demons blocked my way, keeping me for him.

"I will never join you." I crossed my arms and stood my ground, hoping Seth would back down, but he only moved closer, invading my space.

"I don't think you understand. It's not all that bad. Choosing to serve our Lord is not a choice between good and evil, it is a choice to be yourself and enjoy the world as it is. No one will stop you from interfering with humans. There are no punishments, no rules, only that you enjoy the pleasures of humanity."

"Only renounce where I've come from, who I serve, and my home."

"My sweet Arianna, don't you realize that time is ticking way too quickly for you now? You searched for something good and true here. True love. I did everything to stop you, but still you're here with him. And true love's kiss hasn't broken your curse. Nothing you've done has been good enough for them to take you back. It doesn't have to end this way. You're still an angel—at least partly—for the next few hours. Before the clock runs out, you can choose to serve a stronger power. Use that free will of yours to make a different choice."

"Arianna?" Griffin's voice yelled from behind, his footsteps pounding hard in our direction.

I turned. "Griffin, go back inside."

But he'd run too quickly to heed my warning and was already at my side. Seth snapped his fingers and two demons grabbed him by the arms, holding him back.

"What's going on, Ari?"

"We've just moved the party outside," Seth said. "Want to play?"

"Leave him alone," I shouted, shoving Seth in the chest and knocking him back a few feet.

He smirked and straightened himself, fixing the cuffs on his sleeves. "Well, that wasn't very divine of you, now was it?"

More footsteps. I turned my head toward them as another demon grabbed hold of Chloe and she yelped.

"Looks like you've got some true-blue friends here. Did you ever think that maybe they were the ones holding you down?"

"Maybe if you had a few decent friends, you wouldn't be so evil."

Seth laughed and his army chuckled along with him. He snapped his fingers again and the entire group fell silent. Then he marched directly in front of me until his breath fell on my cheeks.

"You had your chance." He ran his hand along my arm, goosebumps pebbling across my skin as the fear of what might happen flashed through me. "We could have been so great together. We could have ruled this pathetic town. You'd have been the perfect queen to my beloved kingdom. But I needed you to choose. I needed you to make the choice to serve Hell."

"Don't touch me." I ripped my arm away.

Seth's lips curled into an amused smile. He walked

back toward the dumpster and squared his shoulders to face me. "Maybe it will be easier if we get rid of a few of these obstacles." He glanced quickly at Griffin and then Chloe. He placed his hands in front of him a few inches apart, palm open to palm, and closed his eyes. Sparks of red and silver exploded between his hands, building and building into an orb that rotated hypnotically between his fingers. He widened his hands as the orb grew. The sparks brightened in intensity and fury.

Seth whipped his eyes open. "Normally I'd let you pick who you wanted to lose first, but tonight, all dressed up like this, I'm feeling like a gentleman. So I guess it's ladies first."

He pivoted in Chloe's direction and pulled his elbow back. The orb flowed with his hand.

"No!" I screamed and ran toward her, jumping the last few feet to knock her out of the way. The orb landed squarely in my chest.

My entire body writhed and twitched as my flesh jolted with electricity. Incredible burning. Shouting voices dropped away in the distance against the loud ringing in my ears. Then everything brightened, lights filtering in. White, pure light streamed around, as if it were the middle of the day. And then as quickly as it began, the pain stopped.

$\mathcal{M}$y hand smacked the marble floor. The sound reverberated into the air as a cold jolt shot through my knees. The downy softness of feathers brushed the backs of my arms, surrounding me, hiding me from the outside, until I caught my breath and chose to stand.

"The doubtful Arianna has returned."

Raguel stood before me, his arms outstretched. The blue radiance emanating around him was nearly blinding after seven days without its brilliance.

"You mean, that's it? It's over?"

Raguel walked forward and placed his hands on my biceps. A blissful feeling spread over my body from where his fingers touched my skin. The gold tips of his feathers shone brightly as they brushed up against my stark white ones.

"Yes, my child. And with hardly any time to spare."

I shook my head. "I don't understand."

Raguel laughed. "You finally demonstrated that you understood the human condition. The feeling of love, unconditional. You sacrificed yourself to save that girl because you cared for her. You put the safety of those humans above your own. You exercised your free will for something bigger than yourself, for no reward, but risking dire consequence. You have proven yourself, and now you may return to the Kingdom of Heaven as you so rightfully deserve."

"Are you saying this was all just a test? That you sent the demons to follow me? To threaten my friends?"

"Of course not. We don't negotiate with their kind. That threat was very real and will be swiftly dealt with. All of this has been on your own."

I shirked out of Raguel's grip and paced up and down the hall. Other angels looked on, not daring to speak, only whisper.

The scene played out in my head—the danger we had all been in only moments before. But with me gone, what would happen to Chloe and Griffin? I doubted that missing the chance to capture an angel would go unrevenged.

"Why do you look so upset? I would think that reclaiming your wings would make you more grateful."

"But what about my friends? The danger was real, and the demons are working on their own orders. What will happen to them?"

Raguel's face fell and he turned his back. His wings curled over his shoulders. "I suspect they will die."

"Suspect? You never guess at anything. You know. They are still in danger, aren't they?"

He refused to turn, but I stormed around to face him as the truth burned bright across his red-tinged cheeks.

"You can't let that happen. You have to save them."

"You know I can't interfere like that. It is not how free will works."

"They wouldn't have chosen to go out there if it wasn't for me. We've already interfered. We need to fix this."

Raguel shook his head and reached out his hand toward me. "Arianna . . ."

"Don't." I raced to the far end of the hall and ripped open the great wooden doors, but before I could take a step out of the court, Raguel's hand appeared at my waist and turned me around.

"What are you doing?"

"You know exactly what I'm doing. If you won't help them, then I will."

"Have you learned nothing? Interfering in the lives of mortals is what brought us to this position in the first place. Don't continue to make the same mistakes."

"This would not be a mistake. And I would be willing to pay any price for my actions."

A hot flood of tears streamed down my face, and I rubbed them with the back of my arm. His expression melted. The stern, steely glare softened, and his lip twitched as his composure wavered.

"You don't know what you're asking. A second offense would not be let off so easy. The consequences would be much more permanent."

"Then do it. Send me back. Give me the chance to save them."

"This wouldn't be a temporary fix, Arianna. I don't

think you fully understand what you're asking me to do."

"But I do. Make me human, Raguel. Please."

Tears filled in the corners of his eyes, but he willed them down, his resolve always much stronger than mine. He placed his hands on the sides of my face and laid a small chaste kiss on my left temple. He let out a deep sigh then turned and glided to the front of the court.

"Very well. As you have requested, shall it be done."

"Thank you," I whispered.

Raguel raised his hands to the sky. His wings stretched out, looking bigger than I had ever seen.

"Wait—" I shouted, and Raguel reverted to normal size. "I need something first. Chloe's mother. I promised, if I returned, that I would find her and tell her that Chloe is sorry."

"You'll waste your last breaths as an angel on this human?" His laughter boomed through the court, a choir of angels joining him.

"Of course. That's what friends do."

His eyebrows raised as a knowing smile graced his lips. "Then the message shall be delivered. I wish you luck, Arianna."

Raguel nodded his head solemnly and the heavens began to spin. Light, color, warmth, all in a familiar vortex as I started to slip away. I gripped the edges of my wings, knowing it was the last time I would feel the comfort of their softness between my fingers. The light dimmed, closing in around me, and I waited for the trauma as I began to fall. Maybe I'd made a mistake. Maybe I didn't need to do this. But as the light faded faster, my heart swelled, knowing this was what I truly wanted. Chloe and Griffin needed me to save them from Seth, but I needed them even more. I wanted to be human with them. I just hoped I wasn't too late. I closed my eyes and bit the inside of my cheek until nothing remained but darkness.

27

*P*ain.

Seth's blast knocked me straight in the chest. The moment of impact. Back to the exact second Raguel had ripped me out of this world and back into my own. Dropped back here as if I hadn't missed a beat.

The magic burrowed under my ribs, spreading toxic through my bloodstream and out into my limbs. I screamed—I think I did—unable to feel my vocal chords stretch and rip but hearing the sound echo all around me. I fell to the ground, arms twitching, as the poison took hold.

"No!" Griffin yelled, but he seemed far away and distant.

Seth stood over me, glaring down at my writhing body on the pavement. His face appeared to smile but with the haze over my vision, I wasn't certain.

"I told you to take the easy way. I never wanted it to come to this."

Suddenly my back arched off the ground. A searing heat ripped through me, battling against the pain.

"What the hell?" Seth stepped back but not quickly enough. The spot Seth had hit—the bullet hole of hate—began to glow. White and blue light streamed out in thick beams illuminating the night. The faraway scream echoed again.

I tried to sit up, but the force pushed me back down. The heat bubbling in my blood intensified, burning all Seth had shot at me and repurposing it into light. He grunted as the beam widened, brushing over him and several of his front-line demons. The agonizing shrieks scarred my eardrums and I grabbed the sides of my head, half expecting it to explode from pressure. Feet pounded pavement—the rest of the minions smart enough to run.

The heat kept building and building, my pulse pounding unnaturally in time until it finally bubbled over, a band of sonic white ripping across the parking lot and disappearing into the world. My body collapsed. My elbows and shoulders scraped the concrete, adding to the sharp agony still lingering in my bones.

Griffin rushed over, the smell of apples hovering above me, his face sharpening in my watery view as he inched his face closer to mine.

"Ari, are you okay?"

"I don't know." But I was alive. A small miracle after facing Seth's firepower. At least Raguel had given me one last gift for letting me go.

His face moved in and out of focus and he put his hand on my cheek, the warmth of his palm easing a fraction of the ache. "Stay with me, Ari. It's going to be okay. I won't lose you now."

I leaned into his touch, begging for it to hold me together. My mind raced as my eyes flickered around, waiting for another face that never came.

"Chloe?"

Griffin didn't speak. Instead he nodded toward the space behind me.

I turned my head, every muscle begging me to stop, but I needed to know. Five feet away Chloe lay on the dirty ground.

"Chloe!"

I rolled onto my stomach and dragged my body the distance between us until I could wrap my hands around hers. Griffin rushed over and placed his fingers at the base of her neck.

"She's breathing."

The weak rise and fall of her chest was the only thing that kept the pain at bay.

"And there's a pulse." Griffin pulled his phone from his pocket. "I need an ambulance. Right away. Faraway High in the back of the parking lot. Hurry."

Voices surrounded us. Questions asked. All combinations of shock—the chaos finally reaching everyone inside and bringing the crowd to us.

I gripped Chloe's hand tighter and inched forward to rest my head on her chest. "You can't leave me, Chloe. I promise I won't leave you. Ever. But you can't leave me. I need you. I can't do this without you."

High-pitched sirens wailed between the buildings. People rushed to lift me as I struggled to fight them off. I wouldn't leave her. I said I wouldn't leave her.

Pain pulsed through me, over and over and over, but I held tight to her hand.

"Back up. Back up." A loud commanding voice yelled in the background as white-shirted medics encircled us.

"It's going to be okay," the voice said.

"But . . ." I tried to argue, but the words never came. Just dark, black pain.

28

Beep. Beep. Beep.

The noise pulled me toward it, gradually getting louder as my head started to clear. I forced my eyes open against the weight of my eyelids. Angry florescent lights greeted my sore retinas. Itchy cotton and not-so-subtle hints of bleach surrounded me. And the beeping. The constant beeping. I pushed up on my elbows, my raw skin burning against the mattress, my head swirling with pain and confusion.

"Easy." Griffin's face appeared beside me, his hands on my shoulders helping me back down. "The doctors say you're going to need your rest."

He let go of my shoulder and brushed his finger across my cheek, sending a pleasant tingle down my back, a release from all the painful ones shooting around my skeletal system.

"So, I'm alive?"

He chuckled, his dark red lips smiling. I loved that

smile. I hoped I would always see him smiling, never the panic I saw on his face when Seth had attacked.

"Yes, and you don't know how relieved I am to know that."

I slid my hand up and caught his near my face, twisting my fingers with his. "I'm pretty happy about it too."

His gaze softened. The waves in his eyes no longer pounded the shore, just a blue expanse of peace glittering in the sun. He leaned over and pressed his lips against mine, the sweet taste of him a temporary balm against my ailments.

"Please don't tell me I have to watch you guys. Maybe I'd rather still be unconscious." Chloe's voice rang from across the room. I turned my head and Griffin stepped out of the way. From her own uncomfortable bed, in her own uncomfortable gown, Chloe sat looking over at us with a playful grin.

"You're okay?" I blurted and tried to push myself up again. The vertigo overtook me, and Griffin settled me back down.

"Of course. You'd miss me too much."

"Yeah, I would."

I wanted to jump from my bed and run across the room and squeeze her until she couldn't breathe, but that would have to wait. There were too many things we needed to discuss with far fewer witnesses. Near the window, Stephen sat in a blue chair, his arms crossed and his head hung in sleep.

"Griffin, would you mind going to get me some water?"

"Anything. But don't think you're getting out of explaining to me what happened." He glanced over at Chloe and back at me, giving me a quick kiss on the forehead before exiting into the hallway.

"Are you really okay?" I asked.

"Yes, I am. All thanks to you." A dark expression fell over her face. "But it's Sunday. If you're still here that means . . ."

"I'm not an angel anymore." I stretched my arm over my back and traced my shoulder blade with my fingers. No scars. No marks. As if my wings had never been there. "Yup. Definitely a human."

"Well, unless you have other plans, you are welcome to stay with me and Dad as long as you like."

"Thank you. I'd love that."

"What about Seth? Do you think he'll come back for you?"

"I don't know. But I doubt it. If I'm not an angel, I'm not worth much to him anymore."

"His loss. I kind of think you're worth more as a human than an angel anyway."

"Maybe. And I'm sorry but I'll never be able to give that message to your mom. I asked Raguel to try, but I don't know if he'll do it."

"That's okay. Maybe she's watching over me up there. Maybe she already knows."

The sun streamed brighter through the window, illuminating the dark corners of the room with the glittery sparkle of hope. Stephen snorted and jostled in his chair until his head fell forward again and back to sleep. Chloe chuckled and I rested my head back on my pillow, watching the rays paint pictures on the ceiling. The tips of my fingers grazed something smooth and soft. I gripped tighter and pulled a perfect white feather out of the mass of hospital blankets. My body relaxed as I brushed my finger along the edges.

"Maybe. But I think she'll get the message."

DID YOU ENJOY FALLING?

If you enjoyed this or any of my books, please consider leaving a review or recommending it to a friend or library. A few moments to spread a positive word can be huge for an author, plus it makes me smile :)

ALSO BY SCARLETT KOL

Never miss a new release from Scarlett Kol by signing up for her newsletter at www.scarlettkol.com.

Dystopian

Mercury Rises

Paranormal

Wicked Descent

Keeper of Shadows

ABOUT THE AUTHOR

Born and raised in Northern Manitoba, Scarlett Kol grew up reading and writing about things that make you want to sleep with the lights on. She believed that the treasures in her mother's jewelry box were magic amulets that would give her immeasurable power and old books could transport her to secret worlds. As an adult, not much has changed. Connect with Scarlett on social media or on her website www.scarlettkol.com.

facebook.com/scarlettkolauthor

twitter.com/scarlettkol

instagram.com/scarlettkol

bookbub.com/profile/scarlett-kol

71725962R00112

Made in the USA
Columbia, SC
02 September 2019